The Gortons of Greenock

Jenny Telfer Chaplin

Published by Kinnon Enterprises Ottawa

ISBN: 978-0-9698825-6-5

ONE

Greenock, Friday April 7, 1820

As Etta Gorton made her way down the outer stairway, the rutted communal steps which served the myriad of closely-packed single-end homes, each filled to bursting point with bairns, she was aware of the usual sounds, smells, and ongoing human dramas of her Greenock tenement building. Six o'clock in the morning it may be, but with the everlasting pressures of trying to scratch a living, the limitations of their overcrowded rat-ridden hovels, and the vocal and insistent demands of hungry weans, nobody ever slept late in Mince Collop Close. Picking her booted way over the broken cobbles, Etta headed along the Vennel, past Herring Street finally into Ropework Street and past the Highland Mary Tavern.

A cursory glance at the portrait-bearing lamp which hung over the doorway of the drinking howff gave Etta a moment's pause for reflection. With this romanticised visual portrayal of Mary Campbell, Rabbie Burns's very own Hielan Mary, her beauty would last forever.

Even better, Etta thought with a bitter smile, *Mary Campbell's life with all its high drama is now safely over. She's at rest. But for me, ma life's struggles are still ... uch tae hell wi it all...*

Shrugging off her dark thoughts Etta hitched up her skirts and with determined strides made her way into her workplace.

The Greenock Ropework Company had been started in 1796 in East Regent Street by Alexander Tough. Fourteen-year-old Etta and her fellow workers didn't give a tuppenny dam for who had established the accursed place. Their sole concern was that for their daily labour the Greenock Ropework Company provided the wherewithal to keep body and soul together. In Etta's case to stave off hunger for herself, her work-shy, drunken father, and the tribe of now motherless younger brothers and sisters. Even so, as Etta slaved away at her own designated tasks she often had the bitter thought: *The man who started up this damned Ropework was well named – it's bloody tough work for weans like me, working our fingers tae the bone for a pittance o hauf-a-croon a week.*

Another day's work in the noise, heat, and frenetic activity of the Ropework over, Etta trudged her way homeward. Normally it was a case of head down and make for home as fast as her tired aching limbs could manage in eager anticipation of the welcome mug of tea which she had trained young Tina to have ready for her. However, her workmate Aggie over the noon break had whispered vague warnings about 'troubles' in the streets that day after work and Etta was much more alert than usual keeping a weather eye open for any sign that might be the signal for her to run tired though she was.

She gave a sigh of relief rounding the corner of Sugarhouse Lane.

"So much for Aggie's gloomy rumours. Now for that mug of tea."

Next morning, Etta more alert than usual, still mindful of Aggie's warnings, thought the streets were, if anything, quieter than normal.

Funny, though, she thought, *what people that are about at this hour all seem to be huddled into wee groups whispering. Ah wonder what about? Uch weel, nane o ma business – best get yersell tae the Ropeworks, ma girl, and damned quick aboot it.*

Angus Duff, the gaffer, gave Etta a sour look as she panted in, just in time to avoid having her already meagre wage docked as punishment for late arrival.

"If it was up tae me," Duff said, as Etta hurried to join the other girls already working furiously, "It's no the Radical Leaders Ah'd be flingin intae Greenock Jail this day. No, mair like a wheen o lazy good for naethin, daft wee lassies that cannae even get oot o their scratchers in time for an honest days work."

Who or what were the Radical leaders? Etta wondered. *Why would anyone want to throw them in the Greenock Jail?*

The morning passed surprisingly quickly and Etta sped home for her midday scrap of bread-and-dripping only to be greeted by: "God help us! Is that ye looking for tae be fed again?"

Since Etta was the family's sole breadwinner there was no answer to this surly comment from her bone-idle, often drunken father. At least not one which would not instantly reward her with a kick from his booted foot.

Despite Etta's stoical silence Tam Gorton went on: "Listen tae whit Ah'm tellin ye ... when ye come hame the nicht for once in yer stupid life use yer heid."

Completely in the dark as to what her father was talking about, Etta took the coward's way out and simply nodded her head, hoping his next words might enlighten her.

"Jist get hame by ony roonaboot way ye like, but make damn sure ye keep well clear o ony streets near tae the toon centre. And for the love o God dinnae get within spittin distance o the Bloody Bridewell. Noo, ye got that, huv ye?"

Again Etta simply nodded.

"Mark ma words, sure as hell roasts the souls o the damned, there's gonnae be trouble in the streets o Greenock this nicht. Trouble the likes o which we've never seen afore. The workers and decent guid-livin folks hereabouts willnae staun for the militia bringing yon political prisoners intae our midst and trying tae lodge them in the Bridewell."

At Etta's blank look, Tam Gorton shook his head. "Uch, see ye ... ye're that dizzy at times ye widnae recognise ony Radical Marchers even if they bashed ye ower the heid wi one o thon banners – Scotland Free or a Desert – whatever the hell that means. Just for once in yer life, bloody well dae what Ah'm tellin ye."

Although somewhat alarmed by her father's warnings Etta thought: *Rough and ready he might be but he must indeed love me if he's all that worried about ma safety.*

These warm comforting thoughts were immediately squelched as Tam continued: "Let's face it – if onythin was tae happen tae ye, God alone kens where our next crust would come frae. Wi ma bad back and it bein a wheen o years afore ony o the rest o ma weans is earnin, without yer Ropework wage we'd be bloody paupers."

TWO

Still smarting from the latest hammer blow to her already fragile self-esteem Etta worked through the afternoon in a blur of misery.

As she and her friend Aggie were leaving the ropeworks, Aggie said: "What's up wi ye the day, Etta? Ye look like someone's stole yer scone."

Etta laughed. "If ever Ah was lucky enough tae hae a scone Ah'd guzzle it doon that fast that Auld Nick or all his witches frae hell widae be quick enough to snatch it frae me."

Taking hold of Etta's arm Aggie said: "They're sayin the Port Glasgow's Militia is tae be in the toon the nicht. With any luck, we'll mibbe get oorsells a sojer. That would soon enough cheer ye up – a braw sojer laddie?"

"After what happened tae Tillie Edgar when she got hersel a sojer – if it's all the same tae ye Ah think Ah'd rather hae the scone."

Aggie pulled a face of mock horror and disgust. "Oh aye, poor Tillie. No a ring on her finger, no a man tae call her ain and no decent-livin body in the toon tae look the road she's on and –"

"And her saddled wi twins no less."

Aggie grimaced. "Trust ye tae look on the bright side, Etta. Niver mind if all else fails we can at least get a good laugh and mibbe hae a bit o a march behind the drummers."

Grabbing hold of Etta's arms Aggie frogmarched her down the street.

"Think aboot it, Etta. If we're marchin alang, surely we'll be safe enough at that? Efter all, they cannae dae the business while they're bangin awa – no at us – but at their bloody great drums. Need tae be damned contortionists so they would."

Mildly scandalised at the turn the conversation had taken both girls took a fit of the giggles. So, helpless with laughter Etta allowed herself to be propelled down the street. When she found them on a street corner furthest from where she had intended to be, Etta jerked free from Aggie's hawser-like grip.

"Sorry, Aggie, but this is as far as Ah go. Fine well Ah'd like tae gae wi ye tae hear the drums but Ah cannae. Ye see, Ah'm takin the lang way hame the nicht."

Aggie pursed her lips. "Oh! Is ma company no guid enough for ye? Is that it?"

At once Etta protested: "Uch, Aggie, nae need tae be sae huffy. Ye're ma best friend. Ma very best friend. Ye ken that. No, the thing is Ah promised ma father ... ye see he was worried aboot me and telt me tae stay clear o the toon centre ...' Etta paused, recalling just how little her father valued her for herself and seeing the hope in Aggie's eyes decided if she was worth so little then she had nothing to lose. "Uch, tae hell wi it. Let's go and look for the drummers. We can dance alang the street wi the best o them. But that's all Ah'm agreeing tae. Mind ye, naethin else ... and o a certainty nae dirty business. Ah'm no Tillie Edgar!"

THREE

Despite dark mutterings from older people on all sides about 'the daft cantrips of young folk', there was still something of a carnival air in the crowded Greenock streets as barefoot, snotty-nosed wee lads, and daft-wi-freedom, newly-released-from-work mill-girls marched towards the sound of drums. However, them aside, the main crowds were of sullenly hostile people and Etta noticed that every small shop she passed was firmly closed, shuttered and in some cases even boarded up.

Perhaps ma father was right after all. Mibbe Ah should hae taken the longer way hame and kept clear o the town centre streets. At this thought and about to change her mind and dart down a side street to head towards the seafront Etta found herself caught up in a crowd which swept her almost to the gates of Bridewell Prison itself.

Marching away from the Bridewell was the eighty-strong company of militia having delivered their five political prisoners into the bowels of Greenock prison. As they attempted to move through the now heaving streets of Greenock, verbal abuse increased in volume and stones, sticks, and even iron bars were thrown at them.

Now thoroughly frightened, Etta and Aggie were borne along like so much flotsam and jetsam by the crowd which was now trying to block the street in front of the militia.

A command was shouted over the hubbub: "Fire! Fire over the heads of the crowd."

In horror Etta saw rifles pointed not into the air but level with the ground and saw the muzzle flash and heard the sound of the volley.

All round Etta men and women dropped like stones. A boy of about eight fell wounded onto the already blood-stained cobbles.

Etta grabbed hold of Aggie and in a blind panic they sought some means of escape. But hemmed in as they were there was no immediate path open to them. At a second volley of rifle fire Aggie lurched free of Etta's grasp and fell.

"Oh, Etta! It's ma legs, Ah cannae move them!"

Aggie screamed and Etta looking round for someone, anyone, to help her was aware that the crowd which only minutes before had been a dense, closely-packed mass of humanity had thinned dramatically as those still physically able had fled the scene after the second round of gunfire.

Feebly trying to drag Aggie along the street, Etta felt a tug at her elbow.

"Listen, if Ah carry yer friend can ye manage to get yerself safely round to the next street and away from this bloody scene?"

Etta nodded at the young workman. In shock, she almost giggled at the thought that the swear word *bloody* was for the first time ever in her hearing being used in *exactly* the correct way. Aggie's legs were covered in blood and she had touched the wounds then trailed her fingers over her face so that this too was smeared with blood.

"Come on, woman! The mob's going to try to storm the gaol. They *might* get the political prisoners out, but God only kens what other rogues and rapists might get free in the stramash. Let's not waste any more time. We've got to get the hell out of here."

He lifted Aggie and over the top of her tousled hair said: "Ma name's Hector – God knows why ma mother called me that – but ma friends call me Torrie."

Etta stumbled her way along the cobbled street after their saviour to a carter's yard. There Torrie placed Aggie on a handcart.

"This is ma place," Torrie said. "We can wheel yer friend home once the streets round here quieten down."

FOUR

On her way to work on the following Monday morning Etta reflected that she was one of the lucky ones. She was alive, while others lay in the mortuary after the massacre; she still had legs that obeyed her bidding unlike poor Aggie whose lifeless limbs would confine her to a wheelchair or a bed for the rest of her days.

Etta choked back a sob as she sidled past 'Plum Duff' and mentally braced for his usual snide comments about her appearance, her timekeeping and even the disputed quality of her work. For the first time ever 'Plum Duff' after a quick glance at Etta's tear-stained face contented himself with a regal wave in the direction of her work station.

Despite her relief at escaping the normal verbal onslaught, Etta could not resist muttering under her breath: "A body would think Ah'm some kind o eejit that still disnae ken her way aboot this damned place."

But accursed place or not, it still provided the pittance of her wages and Etta knew there was nothing else to do – her heart breaking or not – but to roll up her sleeves and get on with her work. While she worked skilfully enough with her hands she could not control the turmoil of her thoughts as she relived the hideous scene of Saturday's massacre.

In her mind's eye she could still see the boy as he lay dying in the gutter, his head covered in blood; the woman, herself wounded, cradling him and saying over and over: "Jamie, lad, hang on. Yer mother'll be here soon. Hang on, Jamie."

But above everything else it was the piteous cries of Aggie until she lost consciousness when Torrie finally laid her in his handcart. Etta could feel the hot colour rising to her cheeks at the memory of the reception she and Torrie got from Aggie's mother.

"Ah blame ye, Etta Gorton. Oh aye, it's all doon tae ye. If ma Aggie hadnae been cavortin aboot the toon wi ye she'd hae been hame hours ago. Walkin on her ain twa guid legs, no gettin dumped on ma doorstep like a bundle o auld rags."

Etta was still reliving the bitter hurt of this unjustified accusation when she became aware someone was talking to her. Jean Jackson, a waif-like woman of indeterminate age, having a miserable life of her own seemed to thrive on hearing about the miseries of others.

"Ah was just saying, that was an awful thing tae happen tae yer pal, Poor Aggie ... and was it just the one leg that got hurted? Or, God forbid, was it baith o them?"

Etta glared and refusing to discuss details said: "Aggie's lucky tae be alive – in fact, we both are and for yer information Aggie's safe at home."

Jean nodded but never one to be put off persisted: "Aye, but ye havenae telt me naethin. Was it the one leg or the pair o them?"

Struggling to keep her composure Etta gave a grim smile and through gritted teeth said: "What Ah am tellin ye is this: any finer details ye might wish tae ken, ye'll just need tae ask poor Aggie hersel."

Jeans' face brightened. "Here noo. That's a helluva guid idea. Thanks very much. Ah'll just come wi ye the nicht when ye gae roon tae visit Aggie."

Etta opened her mouth to protest but Jean was already walking away, stopping only to call over her shoulder: "Richt, well, Ah'll see ye at the corner o Sugarhouse Lane at aboot seven o'clock."

On the point of cancelling such an arrangement, the thought occurred to Etta that perhaps it wasn't such a bad idea after all.

Safety in numbers and all that sort of thing. Mrs Ross will hardly bawl me out again, especially in front of Jean.

As Etta approached the corner of Sugarhouse Lane in good time for her appointment with Jean Jackson she was not surprised although somewhat annoyed to find that the bird-like waif of a woman was already there and impatiently tapping her booted foot on the cobblestones.

By way of greeting Jean called out in an aggrieved tone: "Ah was beginnin tae think ye wisnae comin."

Refusing this early in the evening to be drawn into a pointless argument Etta let the town clock speak for her. With the last peal of the hour of seven she gave Jean a meaningful look.

"Seven o'clock, we said and so now that it is seven, mibbe we can get on our way."

Jean gave Etta a sour look and tightened her grip on the cloth-covered package she held before her. She caught Etta's glance at the parcel and said: "It's just a wee mindin o pancakes ma mother tossed thegether for poor Aggie."

She let this sink in before adding with a satisfied smirk: "Ah see ye're goin empty-handed."

"No only dae Ah no hae a mother standin bye at the ready tae bake a batch o pancakes, the only thing Ah could offer would be a couple of crusts o bread-n-drippin. Ill or no, somehow Ah don't think 'poor wee Aggie', as ye're determined tae call her, would be overjoyed at such a Gorton delicacy. Now can we get tae the Ross's the nicht or no?"

Etta set off at high speed with Jean trotting to keep up with her.

Serve the fussy nit-picker right. Invitin herself along like this.

FIVE

Friday April 9, 1824

In the four years since the terrible night of the Greenock Massacre Etta had made repeated attempts to heal the breach between herself and her erstwhile friend Aggie Ross. Etta was convinced that left to her own devices Aggie would have been only too pleased to resume their friendship. But try as Etta might, it was to no avail. When it finally came to her not even being allowed across the doorstep of the Ross household – of actually having her way barred by the flesh-drooping arms of Mother Ross – Etta admitted defeat. What made the final rejection even more galling was seeing the simpering, parcel-clutching Jean Jackson being welcomed in as an old and valued friend of the Ross family.

Scarcely a day passed without Etta worrying about the situation and brooding about the injustice of it all and grieving for the loss of her former best friend. Despite her best intentions to put the distressing topic out of her mind here she was, yet again, churning it all over in her fevered brain. Given the darkness of her thoughts and no doubt the glum expression on her face, Etta could not help but realise it was entirely her own fault that she was sitting wallflower-like at the weekly Hielan Dance. Even her usual escort, the faithful Torrie, had momentarily deserted her and was dancing with a raven-haired beauty just lately arrived from the Highlands.

Still deep in the morass of her thoughts Etta came to with a start, aware that someone had spoken to her. She raised her head from the contemplation of her fingernails to find herself looking into the amused eyes of a young man.

After a cough he said: "For about the third time of asking, are ye dancing tonight? Or are ye just going to sit there looking glum – as if somebody had stolen yer treacle scone?"

Immersed in her memories, the young man's use of the very common phrase about 'someone stealing yer scone' immediately triggered painful thoughts about Aggie and the Massacre.

Etta stared at the kilted would-be partner before her and snapped: "What did ye just say?"

Obviously unaware he was treading on dangerous ground the young man continued: "Ah'm not exactly asking yer hand in marriage, now am Ah? All Ah'm trying to find out is, are ye or are ye not dancing? That's all, nothing more, nothing less."

Etta shook her head to try to clear it. The young man taking this as rejection started to turn away.

"No, wait," Etta said, "Ah didnae mean, no. Give me a minute to gather myself."

Later, as Etta and Bert sat recovering from their exertions in a boisterous Eightsome Reel, over a welcome cup of tea her new found dance partner said: "Aye, it maybe took ye a wee while to get going but once up there on the floor – ye're one hell of a dancer."

Etta beginning to relax, laughingly acknowledged this rare compliment.

At that moment, a young man who happened to be passing, hearing Bert's comment stopped, glared at them, and strode purposefully to where Etta and Bert were sitting. With a menacing look on his face he stared hard at Etta then turned to Bert.

"A helluva dancer did ye say? It's just a pity – a bloody damn shame – the same thing cannae be said for ma sister, Aggie. It's thanks tae precious Etta here that ma wee sister's dancing days – no tae mention her walkin days – are well and truly ower."

Bert at a loss for a reply said nothing and the man went on: "A wee word o warnin, pal. Just ye watch that the same Etta Gorton disnae upset yer aipple-cart as weel. That wee madam will look after number one an the Deil take the hindmost."

With a final glare at Etta he stamped off to join his own partner.

In the wake of his departure there was an uncomfortable silence before Bert finally said: "What the hell was that all about, Etta? Ah don't know the chap, never seen him before in ma life, and wouldn't know him from Adam. So why in God's name was he shouting at us?

Etta debated in her mind just how she should tell Bert the tale of Aggie's tragedy, but one thing she was sure of was that she did want to hold on to and encourage any developing friendship with Bert. Even after this short acquaintance she knew that never before had she felt such a monumental stirring of her emotions, such a glow of happiness at being in the company of any member of the opposite sex.

She cleared her throat about to say something, anything that would keep him at her side and delay his departure from her life when Torrie arrived on the scene.

"Etta, lassie, are ye all right? God Almighty, ye look as if ye've just seen a ghost. What is it, ma wee dearie?"

When neither Etta nor Bert said anything, Torrie turned his attention to Bert.

"What do ye have to say for yersel? Have ye tired her out dancing? Ah saw the pair of ye cavorting about like a couple of daft idiots. Ye've danced her stupid. That's what ye've done."

Bert finally squared up to Torrie.

"What is it with the folks in this town? Does ma face not fit or something? Fine, Ah ken well Ah'm an incomer to Greenock, but Ah didn't ask to be hounded off my parent's croft by the Clearance Brigands. And in answer to yer accusation – no! Ah haven't danced Etta her into an early grave. Now, does that satisfy ye?"

"No! Ah'm very far from satisfied with what passed for an explanation. Ye've either done something to Etta or maybe said something to upset her. Ah've never seen her in such a stushie since ..."

Torrie's words faded away and both he and Etta knew precisely the time, place, and event he had been about to refer to. Then with a barely perceptible shake of the head Torrie indicated for Etta's eyes alone that his words should be allowed to remain unspoken.

In the ensuing silence Torrie leant forward, grabbed Etta's hands and raising her to her feet again confronted Bert.

"We'll say no more on the subject, Cheucter man. But one thing ye should try to understand ... Etta Gorton is ma girl. Any eightsome reel birling about she needs will in future be done by me."

Bert nodded in ready if somewhat surprised agreement with this statement of proprietorial rights. Even so, in his own defence, he tried yet again to clarify the situation and his part in it.

"Fine. Ah accept that she's yer property. But just let me tell ye this – it was some other fellow, a stranger who really upset Etta with some weird comment about Etta's marvellous dancing and about his sister, Agnes, or some such name, who can't even walk far less dance. Tell him, Etta, tell him. That's the truth of the matter, isn't it?"

By now more upset than ever, Etta simply nodded.

"Was it one of that Ross clan? Was that who riled ye, Etta?"

Torrie turned to Bert and held out his hand.

"Looks like Ah owe ye an apology, Cheucter m ... er ... Bert. Ye'll still not ken what the hell all this stramash was about, but Etta and me, we ken fine what the Ross brothers are like. Cross any one of their clan and ye've made an enemy for life. So – no hard feelings, pal?"

The two men grinned as they shook hands.

"As for me," Bert said, "If Ah was out of line in dancing with yer girl – perhaps in return ye will accept ma apology?"

By now looking like the best of friends, the two men turned and smiled happily at Etta.

She, however, threw her hands in the air and shouted: "Ah am not yer girl, Torrie Duncan. Ah belong to nae man. Ah am ma ain person, and don't ye ever forget it. Ah belong tae nae man!"

Scarcely were the words out of her mouth than Etta, although still meaning every syllable, already regretted having voiced such a rebellious sentiment in public hearing. The look in Torrie's face spoke volumes of the hurt and humiliation at being thus shouted at by a mere woman. Etta knew perfectly well, in her Scotland, and for all she knew throughout the entire world, the male of the species was lord of all he surveyed and his woman was subservient to his every wish. In Scotland for certain, the poor specimen of manhood who was not totally master of his own household was scorned rather than pitied by everyone aware of the fact.

Etta, as she looked at the two men, realised that her isolated, misguided rallying cry for the liberation of women from the domination of men had somehow united Torrie and Bert and cemented their new found friendship. At the same time she wondered if she had not unintentionally issued some weird sort of challenge to any man hearing it to disprove her wild statement that 'she belonged tae nae man'?

It was Torrie who broke the almost unbearable silence.

"Etta, Ah ken ye're upset the night, but even so, there's no call to be making a spectacle of yersel, It's hardly decent."

Etta drew herself to her full height, took a deep breath and said: "Ah'll tell ye what's no decent. Just because ye helped me on that terrible nicht four year ago, and Ah allow ye tae escort me tae dances and church soirees, it's no decent that ye should hae the right tae claim me as *yer* woman. That's what sticks in ma craw, if ye must ken."

Torrie and Bert exchanged glances and Bert offered his solution.

"It's been quite an upsetting evening for ye, Etta. So why not let yer man ... er ... yer good friend Torrie here see ye home. Surely that would be best. Don't ye agree?"

At these words Torrie took a step towards her and, in his usual proprietorial manner, grabbed hold of her by her elbow in readiness for steering her way from the eyes of interested bystanders and out of the hall.

Realising what was happening and that she was yet again being controlled by a man, Etta jerked herself free of his grasp. She glared squarely in his face as she shouted: "Mibbe ye didnae understand me the first time, Torrie. Ah belong tae nae man! Ah'll make my ain way hame!"

Despite the white heat of anger still burning within her, as she left the hall alone, Etta was aware of the bitter cold of the night air, the menacing blackness of the cobbled wynds, and the shadowy threat of the close-mouths. She shivered and pulled the threadbare shawl closer round her.

Although fully aware of how very much she had hurt and humiliated poor Torrie, she still clung to the belief that, thanks to the rock solid nature of their friendship, he would not allow her to walk through the mid-night streets alone. Knowing and trusting Torrie as she did, Etta was fully convinced that at any time now good old Torrie would come rushing along the street after her, determined in his kindly fashion to take her under his wing and see her safely home to Mince Collop Close.

Some minutes later when Etta heard footsteps and heavy breathing behind her she had no fears about turning to greet him.

It was not good old faithful-to-the-death Torrie. It was a stranger, still panting with the exertion of trying to catch up with her, that stood before her. The face seemed somehow familiar – then it dawned on her. This man had been standing nearby and had glared at her rallying cry of 'belonging tae nae man'.

His muttered words of menace: "It's a bloody good job she's no ma woman. If she was, Ah'd bloody well teach the stupid bitch who the Hell she does belong tae," came back to Etta with utter clarity and she cast about in desperation for any passersby.

Not a single soul was to be seen. The only sound was the lonely, mournful cry of a ship's hooter as it made its way along the waters of the Clyde.

SIX

Wednesday May 26, 1824

For long days, and weeks after the assault, Etta could not rid her mind of the hideous event. Day and daily she relived the disgusting experience to the point where it permeated her entire being. Although she knew none of it had been her fault, never-the-less she felt dirty, debased and of little use to anyone. Discussing her worries with friends or workmates was totally out of the question. She refused to let the precise word for what had been so viciously inflicted on her enter her mind. Instead, in her constant regurgitation of the events of that night she thought of it as the 'Attack'. Etta knew that in going over the event again and again in this way she was making herself ill. So ill that now each morning on rising she tended to be violently sick.

As she dragged herself along to the ropeworks Etta couldn't still the thought: *Will this misery never end? Mibbe if Ah could stop thinking aboot that nicht Ah'll stop bein sick and get back tae normal.*

Thursday, June 3, 1824

On their way into work the ever-inquisitive Jean Jackson caught up with Etta and after casting a knowing look at her face said: "Lookin a wee bit peeky again this morning, Etta. So ... not feeling too good?"

Determined not to give even a scrap of information to this pest of a woman Etta waved aside the question. Then, thinking that Jean would persist until she got some kind of answer Etta took a deep breath and said: "Uch, Naethin tae worry yersell aboot, Jean. It's just a summer cold."

Jean, far from being put off, instead gave a crafty side-tilting of her head and stared at Etta.

"Oh my! Is that no lamentable. A summer cold indeed. Mind ye, Ah've heard it cried many a thing, but no that."

Still at a loss as to what her workmate was talking about, in all innocence Etta said: "Aye, that's what Ah said. Since it's of such great interest tae ye, ye'll be pleased tae hear that the whole o oor Gorton clan is sufferin frae it. Ma poor auld father has come doon wi it worse than any o us. Been pukin up his guts for days, so he has."

Jean stopped, threw her head back and gave a great belly laugh.

"Oh my god! Ah cannae believe it – this just gets better aw the time. Listen, hen. If yer father has the same condition as ye ... the auld bastard is goin tae make medical history! There's no another man in the whole world tae match him and that's a bloody fact."

Etta had been so wrapt up in her misery to the point that she was living in a daze, unable, or perhaps unwilling, to accept the harsh reality, the bitter truth of this one particular fact of life.

With the crude jest and maniacal laughter of Jean Jackson ringing in her ear Etta now knew without a doubt that the attack she had endured in that filthy back-court had left her with not only horrific memories but with something more tangible. A consequence which would endure for a lifetime.

When she finally got home after an interminable day, it was to find her father in his usual drunken state, and her brothers and sisters rampaging round the single end. It was all she could do to stop herself screaming and thus adding her voice to the communal uproar.

She could feel stark terror at the very thought of her father finding out that under his roof he was harbouring another Tillie Edgar.

Dear God, she thought, *Ma father would kill me ... bringin disgrace like that on the family. He was aye bad enough leatherin me wi his belt when Ah was younger every time he as much as thought Ah might hae been up tae nae good.*

Later that night as she tossed and turned in the bed she shared with her brothers and sisters, Etta agonised over what she could possibly do before, like the wily Jean Jackson, her father would tumble to the truth of what ailed his family's breadwinner. She fell into a fitful sleep with words echoing and re-echoing like a death knell in her fevered brain: "What in the name o God Ah'm Ah gonnae dae?"

SEVEN

Since the night of the dance Etta had seen nothing of Torrie. If she had thought about it at all, she had assumed with his precious male pride still hurting after her public outburst he was making it his business to steer well clear of her.

It came as something of a surprise therefore when turning a corner towards Sugarloaf Lane and coming face to face with him, he greeted her with a cheeky grin and a welcome such as one might reserve for a long-lost and much-loved friend.

"Hello there, Etta. Are ye not a sight for sore eyes."

"Er ... um ... well, hello, Torrie, Ah must say, Ah'm surprised tae find ye're still talkin tae me."

His grin widened in delight.

"Och, Etta, for heaven's sake, ye surely didn't think that Ah'd let yer daft ramblings about what it means to be a woman turn me against ye. Surely ye ken me a hell of a lot better than that?"

"Oh, aye. That's all very well, Torrie. Words are easy tae say ... but let's face it, Ah havnae seen ye frae that day tae this. Ah was sure ye must hae been avoidin me."

Torrie slapped his thigh in delight.

"Aha, my lassie, ye've given the game away now."

Etta felt a spasm of stark terror and her first thought was: *Oh, Dear God, he knows. He kens what a secret burden Ah'm carryin in ma belly.*

In a hoarse whisper of a voice she hardly recognised as her own she said: "Ah dinnae get yer meanin, Torrie. Just what game would that be?"

Torrie leant against the side of his cart, then hands in his pockets as though settling for a long blether, he looked her full in the face.

'Well, ma dear, if somehow ye got it into yer head that Ah was avoiding ye ... then it stands to reason that means ye must have been looking for me. Is that not a fact?"

Etta felt hot colour rush to her cheeks, but before she could do or say anything to cover her confusion, Torrie went on: Ye don't need to say another word, Etta, Ah can see it yer face. Ye've been hunting the whole of Greenock looking for me. Aye, ye thought ye'd lost yer good man."

Etta raised a hand to push back a stray lock of hair which had escaped its prison of a bun. Only when she had done this to her complete satisfaction did she turn back to Torrie.

"My, my! And are ye no the one with a grand conceit o yersell? Who ever said ye were ma man, guid or otherwise? Ah've never heard such cheek in all ma life."

By now obviously enjoying their repartee Torrie grinned.

"Well now, Ah canae say that Ah see any other man laying claim to ye. So, can ye not just content yourself with what ye're lucky enough to have? Count yer blessings and all that. Let's face it, Ah'm the biggest blessing ye're ever likely to have in yer life, Etta Gorton."

At these words Etta could feel a lump rise in her throat. Trying to fight back tears she said the first thing that came into her head.

"Aye, Torrie, ye hae a grand way wi words. But ye still havenae tellt me this ... if ye're that happy tae see me, how is it that ye havenae been around for weeks on end? No tae put too fine a point on it, Ah havenae seen hide nor hair o ye since that night at the Highander's Ball."

"There's no great mystery and trust me there's only one reason why ye havenae seen me for these last weeks. Anyway, there's the man Ah have to meet about some stuff, so Ah must be off now. Ah'm off again tomorrow for a while, but Ah promise Ah'll see ye when Ah get back and tell ye all about it, Right?"

EIGHT

Tuesday April 13, 1824

The two men meeting in a dockside bar raised a glass to each other. Nodding his sandy-coloured head the younger man said: "Aye, Torrie man. That was some showing up ye got from that lassie at the dance last week. Imagine! Speaking to any man like that."

"A showing up? Is that what ye call it. She bloody-well wiped the floor with me. Come to think of it ... it's well seen ye havenae lived long in Greenock and havenae met many of the lassies from the Tough Ropeworks – tough by name and even tougher by nature. There, doesn't that sum up Etta Gorton?"

Bert nodded. "Aye, ye're right there on both counts. It's true Ah havenae been long here and up yonder in the glens of Sutherland, where Ah come from, there are no women like the ropework lassies. So Ah'm certainly not the best judge of them."

"If there are no harpies like Etta up there it must be a wonderful life. It's a wonder to me that ye ever left such a paradise."

Bert Nairn gave a rueful smile. "Left such a paradise? Do ye honestly think Ah willingly left the life, the people, the places Ah love that are etched into my very soul? No, Ah was thrown out like so much garbage. Out of sheer spite and evil-mindedness the damned wreckers set fire to the sticks of furniture left in the cottage. The brigands hired by the Duke of Sutherland did his bidding. The land was needed, not for honest, decent-living folk working the land, but by his bloody lordship and his diamond-draped lady for sheep. For sheep! Ah ask ye?"

The last was almost shouted out. Bert wiped his eyes, blew his nose noisily and the two sat in silence before Torrie, sympathetic but embarrassed, cleared his throat and gave an apologetic cough.

"After all that, Ah think we could both do with a refill – my shout."

Torrie took his time in returning to their table with the two tankards and rejoining Bert.

"With our common bond against the man-hating lassies of the ropeworks we should be friends – stick together against the common enemy."

Bert nodded and Torrie continued: "Ah've been thinking. Yer tale about honest good-livin folk having to flee from their homes and of necessity having to leave their worldly good behind ... well, while Ah was standing at the bar Ah got a bloody good idea –"

"Listen, Torrie, if ye're about to suggest moving in after the wreckers to salvage any abandoned goods – a filthy scheme capitalising on other folks misery – we'll part company now."

Bert put his tankard down and made to stand.

Torrie put a hand on his arm.

"Ah'm a carter not a graverobber. Just sit back down and hear me out. Anyway from what ye've said, by the time the brigands have done, there's nothing left worth saving. It's all burnt to a cinder or left out in the rain and wind to rot."

"Aye, that's so and the Duke's men wouldn't let ye near anything worth saving while they're about. So, just what do ye have in mind?"

"If we knew a bit ahead of time of crofts that are to be targeted for eviction, do ye think that the crofters might sell some of their bits and pieces? That way they would have some silver to sew in their clothes. Something valuable that's easy to carry when they're thrown out."

Bert took a long drink of his ale.

"Aye, ye might have something there. We were tossed out with just the clothes we stood in. We had some stuff that might well have been worth a few bawbees, but we'd no way to carry it, even if the wreckers had allowed us to move it out of the croft."

"Did the wreckers themselves not try to take anything?"

"Maybe something they could stuff in their pockets, but nothing big. They were on foot or on horseback. Anyway their job was to throw us out and make sure the croft couldn't be lived in after they were finished. So they smashed everything and set fires."

"Right, so it would be worth trying my idea? Would ye come in with me? Ye know the country, speak the Gaelic, know the drovers' inns, the ferries, the farm roads. Ah'll provide the money we need to start and the horse and cart to transport our goods. Are ye in?"

NINE

Some weeks after their ale-fuelled discussion Torrie and Bert found themselves far from the bustle of the dirty, cobbled streets of Greenock approaching a small clachan.

To the north of this small cluster of dwellings the ever-encroaching Highland Clearance had already caused much suffering and heartbreak. In such a climate of dread the crofters had begun to accept that eviction from their homes was inevitable and had started to think of contingency plans.

One worried crofter's wife, Mistress McNab, confided to Bert: "The minute Ah hear that the wreckers are anywhere near at hand Ah know what Ah'll be taking with me – apart from the bairns, of course. Ah'll be taking my mother's good brass candlesticks; the clothes we stand up in, with a few bawbees sewn into the hems of my skirt and jacket; the wedding-ring knitted shawl; the family bible; and that's about it."

Torrie waited patiently until Bert translated the Gaelic for him, then said: "What in heaven's name is a wedding-ring shawl?"

"A very finely knitted christening shawl, so fine that it can pass through the small circle of a wedding ring."

"Fine, but ask her what sort of things she would have to leave behind."

Bert turned back to the woman and in answer to his question she launched into a torrent of Gaelic, ending in tears.

"It's the same for everyone in the clachan, she says," Bert translated. "Everyone has some treasured possession – a grandfather clock that's been in the family for generations, a rocking chair lovingly carved by a young bridegroom for his first home, an elegant crib hand-crafted for a longed-for bairn, a carved, bride's hope chest, a chest of drawers handed down from generation to generation. It's all the same to the wreckers, she says, they smash and burn the lot. Anyone who objects or tries to stop them or even tries to rescue some of their own possessions is beaten and left for dead."

Torrie nodded sympathetically then cleared his throat.

"Bert, wouldn't this be as good a time as any to ask her about what we're proposing – to help out financially?"

Bert tugged at his shirt collar and looked decidedly embarrassed but kept a stubborn silence.

"For heaven's sake, Bert. What are ye, a man or a mouse? Get on with the job. Ask the poor woman how she would feel about selling some of her goods and chattels to us. After all, it's not as if we're planning to steal her stuff, is it?"

As his reluctant business partner still said nothing, Torrie scowled.

"For the love o God, Bert, we cannae call off our great plan at this late date. Think what we've spent already – the fares on the cattle ferries, drinks, meals, and beds at a wheen of drovers' inns on our way here. Ah'm well out of pocket. Ah haven't asked ye to put a hand in yer own pocket, have Ah? Ah ken fine well there's not a brass farthing in yer sporran these days."

The only response to this harangue was a sorrowful shake of the head and a rueful grin.

"Look, Bert, nothing would please me better than to discuss the business with the woman myself ..." Torrie shrugged his shoulders. "But as ye ken very well, Ah haven't yer advantage in the matter of languages. With me not having the Gaelic and her not understanding a word Ah say we're getting nowhere – we're on the high road to bugger-all."

Bert knew without a doubt Torrie was speaking the plain, stark truth. If they did not make a profit of some kind he would again be scavenging the back courts of Greenock. Unless he made an effort to make the business work Torrie would be quite justified in abandoning him and making his own way home, saving what was left of the money he had gathered for the trip.

With an apologetic cough Bert turned to the red-eyed woman.

"Suppose we, ma partner and Ah, were to offer ye, this very day in silver, a few bawbees for some of yer sticks of furniture and ornaments that ye'd be leaving behind anyway once the wreckers arrive – what would ye say to such a proposal? Ah mean would it be any help to ye?"

Mistress McNab looked from Bert to Torrie in silence.

Bert shuffled his booted feet as they waited.

Just when Torrie was about to ask Bert to speak to her again, the woman sat up straight, wiped her eyes with her apron, looked directly at Torrie and spoke to Bert.

Impatiently, Torrie waited for a translation.

"She says, what sort of things would we buy," Bert grinned at Torrie, "and would she get a fair price?"

Torrie sighed with relief. He recognised the look in the crofter's eyes. She was prepared to bargain, to haggle. There was a business in this after all.

The Gortons of Greenock

Two days later they left considerably lighter in pocket but with Torrie's cart loaded with a miscellany of the kinds of household goods Mistress McNab had detailed in their first conversation.

By the second week of June, Bert and Torrie arrived back in Greenock with Torrie's cart loaded to capacity. After unloading at the carter's yard they adjourned to the Highland Mary to celebrate.

Well into their cups, Torrie said: "We should make a handsome profit out of that lot. Ah ken at least two customers that'll pay well for the hand-carved chests and the cradles. Aye, we're definitely in business."

"Ah'll certainly be happy to keep on as yer interpreter and be guided by ye as to the value and prices of stuff we deal in. Ye've surely more of a head for business than me."

Torrie put down his pot and scowled. "What are ye hinting at? Do ye mean Ah'm hard-headed in buying and selling? Do ye think Ah'll cheat ye? Ah've advanced some sillar to ye already even before we've sold anything."

"For God's sake, man. We make a grand team. Ah didnae say ye were hard-headed. But if that's what ye take out of what Ah said, it was a *compliment* not an insult."

"Take my advice, Bert. Save yer compliments for the lassies. But while ye're at it steer clear of Etta Gorton. Ye ken fine what she's like when she's roused."

Bert flushed. "What makes ye mention her to me? She's the last woman on earth Ah'd be the slightest interested in."

"Ye're forgetting the way she drooled over ye at that dance – before the big row broke out. Mind ye, Ah suppose a red-headed, soft-spoken Highlander was something of a novelty for her. Anyway, while we're on the subject, dinnae forget Ah saw her first! Mind ye, a lot of bloody good that's done me so far."

Torrie laughed. "Get us another drink if yer sporran isn't glued shut. The day after tomorrow we'll be off north again for more stuff."

TEN

Wednesday, August 5, 1824

Apart from that brief meeting in June, Etta had seen nothing of Torrie. Then, he had hinted he'd be away from Greenock for some time but as the weeks stretched Etta began to wonder if he was ever coming back.

On her way out of the ropeworks after a particularly gruelling day Jean Jackson caught up with her as she left.

"Ah see yer man Torrie Duncan is back in town again. By all accounts he seems tae be daein very well for himself. In business nae less – buyin and sellin stuff he's brought down frae the Hielans."

Although Etta would have been pleased to hear news of Torrie, she was tired, hungry and wanted nothing more than to get home to the luxury of soaking her feet in a bucket of hot salt water. She was certainly in no frame of mind for Jean Jackson's venomous gossiping.

"Torrie Duncan is no, as ye put it, ma man. Ah've nae knowledge nor even the slightest interest in his business. For yer information: Ah havenae got a man. Is that clear enough for ye?"

"Oh? So ye havenae got a man? Is that what ye'd hae me believe?"

Etta turned swiftly away and headed down Sugarhouse Lane. But quick as she was, Jean Jackson was equally quick. She hiked up her skirts and sprinted ahead of Etta to bar her way.

"So!" Jean sneered. "Let's say Ah believe ye. Mibbe it's true enough ye don't hae a man o yer ain *now*, but sure as hell ye must hae had a man o some kind daein the dirty business wi ye at some time. Truth is, hen, ye're beginning tae show. If Ah was ye, and thank God Ah'm no, Ah'd grab the first man that would hae me – and be bloody quick about it."

Etta without replying stepped to one side, but Jean wasn't finished yet.

"Ah buyed Aggie a lovely wee, carved creepie stool for her birthday frae Torrie Duncan. Daein a roaring trade he is. A pity ye let him aff the hook. *He's* a real catch. He won't be a rich bachelor for long."

As Etta already knew, once back in the so called bosom of her family, there would not be a moment's peace – either from the constant nagging of her father, or from the inevitable backfighting and noisy horseplay of her siblings. With this in mind and with her head churning with the news that Jean Jackson had thrown at her: "Ye're beginning tae show, hen," Etta decided to delay as long as humanly possible her return to Mince Collop Close.

The Gortons of Greenock

Without conscious thought she walked on and next came to her senses to find that she was sitting in supreme isolation on a bollard on the Greenock quayside. Like a soup pot just past simmering, Etta felt her churning emotions and fears were fast approaching the boiling point. Uppermost in her seething mind was the frantic thought: *If Ah am beginnin to show what Ah carry in ma belly then it's just a matter o time before the world and his wife – no to mention ma drunken father – see clearly what Jean Jackson now sees. Oh, god help me. When that day comes ma life is ruined – if ma father disnae kill me first.*

Etta burst into wild, uncontrollable tears.

God in Heaven, Ah'll just be another Tillie Edgar to be mocked and despised throughout the town. Cast out from family, friends, and mibbe worst o all, shamed and castigated before the whole o the church presbytery. A dirty sinner, a pathetic fallen woman sittin perched on the confession stool. Oh, there's no doubt about it, ma father will kill me.

After another long bout of weeping Etta's mind seemed to clear. She knew exactly what she must do.

Aye, Etta, ma girl, there's only one thing to do, Just one thing and be bloody quick about it. It's staring ye in the face.

She found herself standing at the very edge of the quay staring down into the murky depths of the River Clyde.

Just one more step, one short step, that's all it will take and all yer troubles will be over.

On the point of obeying these compelling inner voices Etta swayed on the brink of certain disaster. Finally, she toppled over backwards instead of forwards into the dark waters below, there to end her days as one more wretched suicide, alone, unloved, beaten by life's storms and struggles, conveniently drowned and claimed to a watery grave by the Clyde.

As she rose from the filthy puddle in which she had so unceremoniously landed Etta thought: *Thanks to ye, Jean Jackson with yer vicious tongue and interfering ways – ye may just have saved my life. What was it ye said? Aye, ye mentioned Torrie Duncan, sneerin, "A good catch, Just a pity ye let him aff the hook. Lost yer chance there, didn't ye, Etta?"*

Etta rose to her somewhat shaky feet, dusted herself off and dried her wet skirt as best she could with her handkerchief rag and thought: *So, Ah let Torrie Duncan off the hook did Ah? Well, now, who's to say Ah can't reel him back in again?*

With this banner call to positive action, Etta squelched her way through the dark Greenock streets homeward.

Tomorrow would be another day.

Aye, Torrie ye're not off the hook yet. Ah've a wee spot o fishing to do yet. See if Ah dinnae.

Next day being a Sunday and the so-called day of rest, Etta rose early, cleaned out the spent ashes from the grate, relit the dying embers of the fire then finally made a pot of watery-thin porridge for the family. Then with all the bairns and her ever-irritable father thus fed and watered Etta took time to attend to her own personal needs. As she rubbed at her skin with a coarse face-flannel, as if in this way she could cleanse her body of the horrific mental and physical abuse which she had endured these past weeks, she debated in her mind as to what should, or in fact could, be her best course of action from now on. Then on the point of pinning up her long hair she stopped with upraised arms and a mouthful of bone pins and suddenly in that moment she knew, knew instinctively what she must do if her master plan for her survival were to have the faintest chance of success.

Aye, she thought, *that's what Ah'll do. Ah'll go to the Kirk this very morning.*

With the decision now taken she yet again brushed down her skirt lest there should still be traces of mud left over from her escapade of the previous evening. Having once satisfied herself that there were no tell-tale globules of mud still clinging to the folds of her skirt, she then put on her one and only coat, a poor hand-me-down shadow of once robust tweed. To top off her churchgoing ensemble, she rammed her Tam-o'-shanter with its brave toorie onto the now pinned up hair, the latter a well-skewered prison for her luxuriant hair.

Right! she thought, *That's me. Ah'll show them. Ah'm every bit as good as every single one of those Bible-toting matrons. Keeping up appearances that's the name of the game, Etta ma lass.*

Once out in the street, she strode purposefully along, at the same time as trying to hold on to her outward display of courage and bravado with the thought: *If things go according to ma plan it will be more than worth this effort Ah'm making. And with any luck, even if Ah don't get a chance to speak to him Ah should at least catch a sight of Torrie sitting in his mother's pew. If nothing else it will remind the now high and mighty Torrie Duncan that at least Ah do still exist. So, one way and another, definitely worth a try.*

Later that same day having stoically endured a mind-boringly dirgeful sermon, much to her chagrin Etta realised that she was still no nearer achieving her aim of catching sight of Torrie Duncan. Certainly a quick glance from time to time across at the Duncan's family pew told Etta that while his sour-faced mother was in attendance, and obviously hanging on to every mournful word that fell from the Reverend Mr T. Thompson Murray's lips, of Torrie there was still not a sign. Biting back her bitter disappointment, when the church emptied and the now suitably spiritually uplifted congregation was at last free, Etta rather than spending precious time hanging about to blether with anyone, instead rushed off with as much decorum as she could manage. So intent was she trying to avoid chitchat or social contact of any kind with other worshippers that she kept her head lowered as she rushed along towards Mince Collop Close and she all but cannoned into someone as she rounded a corner. Feeling it to be her fault for having been so careless in unladylike rushing long the cobbled street, Etta at once raised her head to apologise to whoever it was had been the recipient of her clumsy actions. The ready apology froze on her lips when she found herself staring into not one but two pairs of eyes.

One pair belonged to the very person she had been scheming to meet but the other pair belonged to that *other* man who had been much in her thoughts lately. The three young people stood laughing and staring at each other surprised at meeting thus on a wind-swept street corner.

"Etta Gorton! Fancy bumping into ye."

Etta felt hot colour rushing to her cheeks. *Bert remembered ma name! And that from only our one meeting at that dance. He remembered ma name!*

Torrie laughed and slapped Bert on the back. "From the look of it she's really pleased to see us. Just look at her blush. If she has designs on ye, Bert, trying to get her hooks into ye, ye'd be hell of a lot safer away from her womanly wiles up yonder in the frozen wilds of yer Sutherland glens."

Afraid that the mounting colour in her cheeks had indeed betrayed her feelings for this comparative stranger – feelings of love and adoration which she could neither understand nor explain to herself – Etta decided that attack was the best defence.

"Oh, and do ye mind if Ah ask the both of ye just what makes ye think Ah'd look the road either o ye was on? Far less, as ye so coarsely put it, get ma hooks into ye. Is either one o ye eejits supposed to be a great catch or something?"

"Aye, lassie," Torrie said, Ah'll give this; ye don't change much do ye? Still beholden to no man. Still belong to yourself alone, that it? Do ye never get tired of beating away at that same old drum?"

Refusing to be drawn any further into a pointless war of words, Etta tossed her head, all but dislodging her Tam-o-shanter, and taking a firm grip on her Bible turned away.

She was about to walk on when Torrie said: "No need to take umbrage, Etta. We're just having a bit of harmless sport with ye. After all, it's not as if ye were some poor, shilpit, feeble woman that couldnae stand up for herself, or say boo to a goose, is it"

When Etta made no reply, Torrie went on: "Listen, if ye're not still in the huff by then, we'll maybe see ye at the Highlander's dance on Saturday."

Etta walked on without answering him, but it was all she could do to stop herself smiling in triumph. Torrie had said, "We", so if both of them were to be there, perhaps after all, she could set her cap at the fresh faced Highlander.

On her way home feeling as she was walking on air, Etta could still recall that first sensation of excitement and exhilaration when she had danced with Bert.

Yes, she thought, thinking of the openly admiring glances Bert had bestowed on her at their recent meeting, *the spark between us is real enough. It's not just my imagination.*

Hardly daring to allow herself the luxury of such a wonderful dream, she whispered into her coat collar: "Bert Nairn? Oh aye. The very dab. Ma bonnie wee Highlander would do me just fine. Just fine."

By the time Etta and her cousin Jinty arrived at the Saturday night dance with Jinty's husband the dance was well under way and Etta could see no sign of Bert Nairn. She did, however, spot a red-faced Torrie in full flight swinging his partner around the dance set. He in turn caught sight of Etta and in his usual cheery, hail-fellow-well-met manner he let go of his dance partner with one hand and gave Etta a friendly wave and a cheeky nod of his head.

One of two gossiping matrons sitting near Etta said: "Isa, see that chap that's waving to somebody and wagging his head like the town's Daft Dunkie? Well, if that's who Ah think it is, then there's damn all daft about him."

Her friend craned her neck to see who was meant. "Aye, Ah see him, making funny faces now, He disnae look the full twenty shillings to the pound, to me."

"Making money hand over fist he is. Him and some red-headed fellow from up North that he's teamed up with. Sellin bits and bobs o knickknacks, furniture and stuff that they bring down from the Hielans. That's the story anyway. Mind ye, Isa, ye ken as well as Ah do ... what they don't know for a fact in Greenock they make up."

Isa sat up straighter. "Funny that. Ah can set ye straight on the story. Ye ken that woman Ah clean for – the wife o yon high heid yin from the Sugarhouse – just the other day she spent near enough a damn fortune buying some scooty wee hand-carved chairs and a grandfather clock. Ah couldn't figure out where in Greenock she could buy them, but now it's all clear."

Her friend didn't look too pleased at having her story capped and went on: "Well, isn't it good that Ah told ye about them fellows. Anyway, ye mark ma words, some lassie will soon be setting her cap at one o those two braw lads."

Isa laughed. "Ye're right there. With siller like that in their pockets, they'll not be carefree bachelors for long ... not in Greenock anyway."

Having shamelessly evesdropped on the conversation between the two matrons Etta felt a flutter of fear. Doubtless both matrons had marriageable-age daughters of their own still to find suitable and hopefully solvent husbands.

Ma master plan o getting my hooks into Bert or Torrie maybe isn't going to be as easy as Ah thought. If they're goin to have the pick o the women in Greenock Ah'd better put ma best foot forward and pretty damn quick about it before it's too late for me.

Etta was still deep in thought when, with a start, she realised that Torrie was now purposefully making his way across the room towards her.

With a mock serious lordly bow he said: "If it wouldn't upset yer ladyship's sensibilities too much, would ye consent to having a dance with me – a mere man?"

Despite herself, Etta laughed, so loudly that it caused the two gossiping matrons to pause their conversation in mid sentence and give Etta a cold, fish-like stare.

As much for sheer devilment as for gaining information for herself, Etta flashed Torrie her most flirty smile.

"No sign of yer other half tonight? Where's the trusty Bert? Ah thought ye two were joined at the hip."

Torrie stared at Etta for a moment before roaring with laughter.

"Steady on there, Etta. If Ah was ye Ah'd watch how Ah went about the town saying dirty things like that. Folk hereabouts have led sheltered lives. Hearing the likes of that they might get the wrong end of the stick – and it would be one hell of a shock for them."

Puzzled as to what Torrie was talking about, and what it was that she'd said that was in any way rude or could be construed as 'dirty', Etta took the coward's way out and smiled sweetly.

"Ah don't know what flights o fancy ye're on about now, Torrie, but in simple language what Ah'm askin ye is where's Bert tonight? Ah thought, in the normal way o things, when he was in Greenock he never missed his Saturday night ceilidh at the Highlanders."

Torrie coughed and cleared his throat. "Etta, Bert Nairn won't be coming here tonight for the simple reason that Ah told him to make himself scarce and give me a fighting chance. After all Ah'm the one that saw ye first."

Etta opened her eyes wide at this unexpected news. "Is that a fact, Torrie?"

"Now, Etta, are ye dancing? Or are ye going to stand there all night like a stookie at an Irish wake?"

In that moment Etta knew it was decision time and not just about the question of dancing. Bert Nairn was beyond her reach as possible husband material – the dye was cast. Fixing her most entrancing smile on Torrie she said: "If ye're asking, then aye, of course, Ah'm dancing. Lead on McDuff."

ELEVEN

These days Torrie was as proud as any man could be. Not only was his business enterprise succeeding beyond the limits of his finest dreams, but also amazingly Etta Gorton had consented to be his wife.

As the day of the wedding approached with each day that passed far from looking the picture of a bonnie bride Etta's face appeared more worried and ashen.

Thinking to cheer her up and perhaps put some more colour in her cheeks, one evening as they strolled along the locally designated 'Lovers' Lane' by the waterside Torrie said: "There's no need for ye to get yourself into a stushie of nerves about the wedding feast and all that. Everything will be just fine. My mother is a great organiser."

At the mention of his mother Etta could feel the muscles of her face tighten.

A great organiser, oh aye there's no doubt about that. But Ah'm sure she'd far rather be organising a different kind o bride for ye. One o the spinsters o the parish – from the church choir – one o the genteel bodies that doesn't work at the Ropeworks. Good works among the poor, mibbe teaches elocution for her pin money. Aye, that's the kind o bride she'd rather have for her precious Hector Cameron Duncan, son of a sea captain, now dead.

Etta shook herself alert at once aware that Torrie had said something.

"Etta, Etta! Ye were miles away. Ye've no need to worry. Ah've told ye, everything will be just fine. Ma mother will see to it all. Even my Aunt Euphemia is so pleased that Ah'm getting married that she's baking a cake for the big day."

Etta gave a wan smile. "Aye, Torrie that's good to know."

"Right then put all that stuff out of yer head. What about a wee kiss for yer soon-to-be-husband?"

As Etta proffered her cheek for a chaste kiss she had a fleeting moment of panic.

Ah'll never be able to carry this off. What in God's Name have Ah got myself into in accepting Torrie's offer o marriage? If Ah'm being honest, not only can Ah barely thole his mother, Ah hate the sight o his Aunt Euphemia, and though Ah like Torrie as a good friend the thought o him as a husband scunners me even to think o it.

Oh God, the minute he finds out Ah've cheated him with a bairn on the way there'll be bloody hell to pay.

Two mornings after their walk down lovers' lane Etta was stunned to notice a stain on her clothing. Almost in a state of collapse she looked in utter astonishment at the undergarment she held in her trembling hands.

No! It can't be, can it? Ah don't believe it – after all this time? Not after all the connivin, flirtin and schemin Ah've had to do to get Torrie to propose marriage.

But the physical evidence was there. It was indisputably, gloriously true – her monthly curse – *Not that Ah'll ever call it that again* – was yet again a definite visible part of her life. Nor was it a pale, weak trickle. No! It was a full-bodied, bloody, scarlet reality in full flow.

At first uncertain as to why it had been absent these past months Etta in a flash of understanding realised that the emotional and physical shock of the horrific attack must have not only stopped the flow, but had also thrown her entire body clock into complete disarray.

But what about Jean Jackson's comment that Ah was 'showing'?

Etta looked down at her undeniably extended stomach.

Yes, Ah've certainly put on some weight. But, thank God, it's not a baby.

As she thought about the question it dawned on Etta that for the past few months she had been eating anything she could lay hands on. Perhaps getting some comfort from scavenging extra food that normally would have gone to her siblings.

So, thank God, Ah'm free! My body's my own again. Ah'm a free woman beholden to no man!

But just as she rejoiced, she crashed back to earth with the thought: *Free? Ye stupid bitch! A short lived freedom with a soon-to-be wedding.*

Etta slumped into the nearest chair. As from the date of the wedding she would no longer be Etta Gorton but Etta Duncan without the right, and perhaps even without the inclination, to declare to all and sundry, "Ah belong to no man."

So much for my fine hopes and dreams o bein a free spirit, free o any man's shackles. Some free life it's goin to be ... not only chained to a man for life, but damned-well married to the wrong man!

Desperately tired though she was, Etta spent another sleepless night twisting and turning, worrying this time not about an unplanned baby but instead about her future,

How in the name of God am Ah goin to tell him? Especially at this late date. All the arrangements are made. His organising mother has seen to that. His damned Aunt Euphemia has baked a cake. Torrie has picked his best man and Ah've even handed in my notice at work. Father is in the huff over that – Ah'll no longer be the breadwinner o the family.

The very thought of the best man gave Etta palpitations. Originally Torrie had asked his cousin to do the honours but he had sailed on very short notice on a long voyage as ship's bosun to New Zealand. Without any prior consultation Torrie had asked Bert Nairn to stand in. At the very thought of standing close to the man she really loved while she married another whom she regarded as no more than a good friend Etta felt her blood run cold in her veins. Come what may she had to get out of this marriage.

A short twenty-four hours ago, while not exactly looking forward to being married, the best man fiasco aside, she had had an entirely different outlook. Torrie had been the heaven sent answer to her prayers – to make the unwanted baby legitimate, to save her from disgrace.

Next morning Etta rose at her normal five o'clock, bleary-eyed, sleep deprived and irritable. In the kitchen to her amazement was her layabout father already seated at the table. Probably the first time in his adult life he had been up at this ungodly hour. Etta knew she was looking somewhat less than her best, but one glance at her unshaven, wreck of a father made her think whatever ailed him on this morning he was looking even worse than usual.

He looked up from his sad contemplation of a mug of tea.

"Ah've had one helluva sleepless night. And no that it'll be any interest to ye, Ah put blame all doon to ye."

Etta paused with the porridge spurtle in her hand and looked questioningly at him.

"Ah'm near dementit with the worry o it all."

"Worry? What have ye to be worried about?"

"It's not every day that a man's daughter chucks in her job and leaves her poor auld father with a brood o starving weans and no prospect beyond the workhouse."

Etta sat in the rickety chair across the table from her father and stared.

That's it! That's how Ah can call off the marriage. The perfect excuse. Ah'll see Torrie tonight and explain. Him bein the gentleman he is, is sure to understand.

"What's happened now? Ye're sitting there grinnin from ear to ear. Have ye heard one word Ah said?"

"Aye, father, don't worry any more. Ah know now, how to set everythin right. Just ye wait and see."

The day seemed endless before the time to meet Torrie finally arrived. All day she rehearsed in her mind how to put matters to him, running through scenario after scenario. Finally she decided the gist had to be: They were being selfish thinking only of themselves. She couldn't leave her father and her siblings with no-one to provide for them. He as a good Christian man couldn't abandon his mother to a lonely, possibly impoverished old age. No, they would have to be brave and considerate and give up their plan to marry.

Etta could never afterwards remember exactly how she finally broached the topic, but eventually she did manage to indicate that Torrie was free of his promise to marry her.

"Ah'll mibbe manage to get them to take me back on at the Ropeworks, but failing that they're always lookin for unskilled girls at the Sugarhouse. That way Ah'll be able to look after father and the weans and he won't have to worry about the threat o the Workhouse."

Etta stopped for breath aware that she had been rambling on and was now in a lather of fear as to how her 'intended' would react to this blow, not only to his romantic hopes, but also, and perhaps more importantly, to his manly pride.

Torrie had been leaning against a wall through her rant. He stood straight, leant forward, put a hand on each of her shoulders and drew Etta towards him.

"Etta! Etta! My darling if it takes me the rest of my life on this earth Ah'll never be able to thank ye enough for what ye've done for me this evening."

Totally confused by this unexpected reaction Etta held herself stiffly away from the would-be embrace.

"Were ye all this while really wantin to escape the bonds o marriage. There's no need to thank me. If ye had wanted to break the engagement before this, ye only had to say ..."

"Break the engagement? Call off the wedding? Not get married to the most wonderful, most thoughtful, the bonniest girl in the whole of Scotland? What havers are ye talking, lass?"

Nerves stretched to the breaking point, Etta snapped: "Havers or not, Torrie. What is it then, in God's Name, that ye're thankin me for?"

Again Torrie drew her close but this time with a more determined grip.

"Silly wee lassie that ye are. Ye're such a good living girl even reminding me of my Christian obligations to honour my mother, just as ye are dead set on looking after yer father and yer brothers and sisters, even though ye think it means giving up yer own hopes of married happiness. Ah just can't get away with how utterly unselfish ye're being. An angel in disguise, that's what ye are."

Instead of meekly offering her cheek for an anticipated kiss Etta again drew back.

"Oh, Torrie, if only ye knew."

"Ah know all Ah'll ever need to know about ye. With what ye've said tonight ye've given me a bloody great idea. Aye, Etta, ye and me are going to make a great team against this cruel world. No-one's going to be sent to the workhouse."

Torrie lunged forward and hugged her.

"Forget any chaste wee kiss. The way Ah'm feeling right now Ah don't know how Ah'll be able to hold out 'til the wedding night. Come here, Ah've waited long enough."

TWELVE

In the wake of that memorable night everything round Etta seemed to happening at breakneck speed. She felt herself being swept along like a piece of flotsam adrift on a raging sea. With each new event she had the strangest sensation of being a complete, and only slightly interested, stranger looking down from some great height at the unfolding of what should have been her own life.

As she entered her home in Mince Collop Close after work she found Torrie sitting across the table from her father. From the jug of ale before them and their completely relaxed attitude they looked like two old friends enjoying each other's company and a good blether.

Torrie turned and smiled.

"Ah, there ye are, Etta. Ah've just been explaining my grand idea to yer father."

Etta felt her lips tighten in annoyance.

"It's about time ye explained yer grand idea to me. Ah've surely got the right to know what ye've got up yer sleeve."

Her husband-to-be gave her a patronising smile.

"Nothing for ye to bother yer pretty head about ... this is man's business."

Etta leant a hand on the table and glared at the two men.

"Man's business? The way Ah see it is this ... if any part o yer great plan involves me, then surely to heaven Ah have the right to know."

Her father frowned. "Ye still don't get it, Etta do ye? As a woman – a mere woman – ye have no rights. That's something, a fact o life, that ye have never been able to understand. Once ye're married yer husband will be yer lord and master. Then it'll be a case o doin what yer good man tells ye to do ... love, honour and obey ... it couldn't be any clearer than that, could it?"

Almost apoplectic with anger and frustration at such a future Etta opened her mouth to reply but Torrie was too quick.

"No need to get upset, Etta. It's all settled and yer father and Ah are both well pleased with the idea. Ye see, yer father has accepted my offer of employment and –"

"Employment? My father doesnae know the meaning o the word, certainly not as applied to himself."

Torrie placed a placatory hand on her shoulder. "That's enough."

She shook off his hand. "Enough is it? Oh aye, ma father always made sure there was cnough work for me slavin away at the ropeworks.

But him soilin his hands with hard graft ... that would be the last thing, the very last thing on God's earth for him."

Looking Etta square in the eye Torrie said: "For the last time, that is no way to speak to yer father. Ah'll not have it. Ah absolutely forbid it. Especially when the poor man, sore back and all, has agreed to work for me round at my carter's yard."

Etta turned away to make her way out of the room, but Torrie's hand restrained her.

"Now then, my girl, ye can like it or lump it, just as ye wish, but be sure of one thing: Ah'm starting as Ah mean to go on. As of this very minute we'll have no more of this female carry-on of flouncing off in a huff when something doesn't please ye. Now then, an apology to yer father, that's what is required. Then ye can make a pot of tea for us – now, that is woman's business looking after her menfolk."

While Torrie and her father had insisted that their proposed plans were exclusively men's concerns, Etta found out soon enough that they rapidly became within a woman's province the very minute that actual hard work reared its ugly head.

The flat above the office at the carter's yard had been empty for some time and as Torrie said: "It will be just grand for yer father and the bairns, once ye have it cleaned out and set up. Apart from anything else yer father as my employee will be able to keep a weather eye on the stuff stored in the yard and the sheds."

"Talk about fallin in the Clyde and comin up with a gold watch. Yer job will suit my father – the lazy lout – down to the ground. Sittin on his bum all day, same as usual, but now a glorified caretaker. It hardly merits the word *work.*"

Torrie pursed his lips in obvious annoyance.

"Come on, Etta. Can ye not just be pleased for the old fellow? After all, he's done a good job bringing up yourself and those bairns of his on his own. There's not too many men would tackle that or would even attempt to be both father and mother to a whole squad of weans. Surely he deserves a bit of luck for once in his life."

Etta felt there was much she could have said on the matter but decided not to enter into yet another slanging match.

"Aye, that's as mibbe, Torrie but ... that wee flat ... Ah had assumed, wrongly it seems, that it would be our home when we got married."

"Well, ye certainly did think wrong didn't ye?"

"It seems a bit of a waste to me, Torrie. Ye can take from me, Ah know his lazy, idle ways. Ma father will have that bonnie wee flat like a tinker's midden in no time at all."

"Ah'm not with ye, Etta. Ye'll be fairly close by and ye'll be able to come round every day and clean out the place for yer father and the weans."

Etta took a step back and faced Torrie arms akimbo.

"Just where will Ah be laying down my own head that Ah'll be that convenient to be a scodgie to them?"

"Ah thought ye'd have guessed by now. When we're man and wife we'll be as snug as two bugs in a rug living in Sugarhouse Lane with my dear mother."

Almost too stunned for coherent thought blurted out: "Yer mother! Dear God in heaven she can't stand the sight of me!"

Torrie laid a placatory hand on Etta's arm. "Oh, Etta, ye've got it all wrong. To my mother ye'll be the daughter she always wanted but never had. And ye'll be able to look after her. She's looking forward to that."

THIRTEEN

The wedding and its attendant celebrations were now well and truly over and Aunt Euphemia's cake now a distant memory. Life had settled to what passed for some semblance of normality. Etta's father and siblings were very much at home in the flat above the carter's yard office-cum-storeroom. In accepting and enjoying his new role as a trusted, capable, and locally respected caretaker Tam seemed cleaner, brighter and somehow now more in charge of his life.

As Etta once again cleaned the flat round him she reflected that while her father's life had taken a distinct turn for the better the same could hardly be said for her own situation.

If this is marriage who the hell in their right mind needs it? Since attainin the dizzy heights of being Mistress Torrie Duncan Ah've got more work than ever. Not only do Ah have two homes to clean, wash and cook for instead of one, Ah've got two men to answer to. Damn it, it's not just two bosses Ah've got three countin Torrie's sainted mother.

Still on her knees scrubbing the floor Etta heard her father say: "Etta lass, Ah've got to hand it to ye. The best thing ye ever did for me was to marry that Torrie lad. Not only does he give me a weekly wage for sitting here nice as ninepence on my bum lookin after the yard, but now he's come up with another grand idea for me."

Etta looked up, pushed a stray lock of hair under her mob cap, and asked with a tinge of envy and weariness: "So, what now, father?"

Tam beamed. "Ye'll never credit it. He told me this morning that he'll give me a wee bit extra silver – Ah can't remember the word he used, comm– something – anyway the top and bottom of it is this ... every time Ah sell any of the sticks o furniture and the like o the stuff he's brought down from the Hielans he'll see me all right for a wee backhander."

With considerably more force that was needed Etta slammed the scrubbing brush into the bucket.

"Ah'm right happy for the pair of ye. Ye make a lovely couple."

The day started like any other in the Duncan household. The Young Mistress Duncan, as Ettta was now known locally as opposed to her formidable mother-in-law, had already been up for some time. Since her self imposed starting time of five o'clock, so far she had made up the fire, prepared and served the morning porridge to Torrie and herself and was now setting out breakfast for her now-bedridden mother-in-law. The latter, who now quite shamelessly revelled in having 'the daughter Ah have always wanted but never had', made sure that the already harassed Etta now attended to her every need.

The young girl who had been the general servant – chief cook and bottle washer – had been summarily dismissed as soon as Etta moved in, as being 'surplus to requirement and a needless expense'.

Old Mrs Duncan had retired to her bed in her upstairs room declaring herself a prisoner to her rheumatics but although she enjoyed having Etta run up and down stairs at her beck and call it made her too isolated from the supervision of the kitchen and the main floor. Torrie solved the problem by bringing in a day bed and setting it up in the large kitchen. So, after her breakfast in bed, once the house was well warmed and there was no hint of damp, Mrs Duncan would descend to the day bed. From there she ruled the household.

Apart from issuing orders she was adept at stirring up trouble and giving her own highly embroidered version of local gossip and that morning ensconced beside the kitchen fire she said to Etta: "My friend Greta dropped in to see me when ye were round at yer father's place the other day. She was telling me about yer father –"

"Oh, is that so? My father's just fine these days, thanks to Torrie, so Ah don't think Ah need to hear any o Greta's ill-informed gossip."

Etta turned back to cleaning the porridge pot, but Mrs Duncan was not to be put off.

"Oh aye, true enough. He is doing well these days. That's the trouble by all accounts. It seems he's the talk of the town."

Well aware that Mrs Duncan wouldn't have raised the matter unless there was some scandal and scurrilous gossip involved Etta sighed. About to speak, Etta stopped.

No, Ah'll not encourage her.

After a silence, Mrs Duncan pushed herself further back against the pillows.

"What's wrong, Etta? Cat got yer tongue? Ah'm sure ye'd much rather hear about your father's daft cantrips from me than from any of the town gossips"

"My! That's real thoughtful of ye, Mother-in-law, to try to spare my feelings. Ah really do appreciate it. Ah'm sure if anybody in the town knows all about my father's antics – whatever the are – it must surely be ye. So let's hear the latest bulletin."

Mrs Duncan gave her daughter-in-law a flinty look, but sarcasm or not it was an invitation.

"It's no wonder that decent good-living folk are all talking about him. It's simply not right the way he's carrying on. Ah mean to say, a widower in his forties with a gaggle of children shouldn't be running himself stupid chasing after women. It seems there isn't a woman or girl safe when he's around."

Determined not to give Mrs Duncan the satisfaction of showing her shock, Etta shrugged.

"Is that all? My father has been chasing women for years, but one lungful of his whisky-laden breath, one look at his bloodshot, bleary eyes and they ran screaming. Ah'll grant ye that he looks a sight more respectable now."

"If ye would just keep quiet for long enough Ah'm trying to tell ye something else. The word on the street is that he's talking of getting married again. Now, what do ye think of that?"

At this Etta was surprised and shocked but still not willing to give ground to Mrs Duncan.

"Ah've known all about that for ages. Now that he's got a bawbee or two in his pockets mibbe some women won't be so fussy about his appearance and habits. Mind ye as Ah said he's looking better now than he's done for a long time. Ah can hardly credit it myself, but Ah hear there's a queue of widow-women all angling for the position."

"Ye've known about this for some time? Some daughter-in-law ye are! Why didn't ye tell me he was in the marriage market? It's not right that Ah should be the last woman in Greenock to know."

"To tell ye the truth, it did cross my mind and Ah did think o passin the word on to ye ... ye bein a widow-woman yerself ..."

Mrs Duncan's face flushed.

"You don't think I would lower myself even to think of union with your father."

"Anyway, he'd be looking for an able-bodied woman – someone who could work her fingers to the bone for him. Not some decrepit, old woman 'a prisoner to her rheumatics'. So ye see Ah didn't tell ye so as not to raise yer hopes."

Her already flushed face now turning crimson Mrs Duncan said: "I know who's ready to grab the old fool, but since you're so smart you can just find out for yourself. My lips are sealed."

The rest of the morning passed in a stony silence before Etta prepared to set out for her father's flat.

If what old Dreary Duncan tells me is correct it seems to me that such a change in father's life could well do me a power of good. Once the old man's safely married he'll have a wife to do his biddin, his cleanin, an unpaid slave to look after his bairns. It'll no longer be any business o mine. All Ah'll have to do is run one house and look after Torrie and his 'invalid' mother. So whoever the lucky woman is Ah'll welcome her with open arms ...

Just as Etta was about to close the door behind her, Mrs Duncan unable to contain herself any longer called out a name – the name local gossip suggested was to be Etta's new step-mother.

No, it can't be right. Ah didn't hear her properly. No, please God they've got it wrong. Not Jean Jackson!

"Ah just don't believe it, Father. It seems the Greenock rumour mongers got it right this time for that is the name that's being bandied around, but Ah just couldn't believe it. Ye must be in yer dotage if that's what ye're planning. All right, get married if ye must, but why her?"

"What's wrong with my bonnie Jean? Just tell me that. Ye seem to think all women have the same warped attitude to men as ye do. My bonnie Jean, fair desperate for a man of her own couldn't accept my honourable proposal o marriage quick enough. She's a decent, good-living, church-going spinster o the parish –"

Etta couldn't contain herself and longer.

"If this is the same Jean Jackson, father, ye've missed out her most attractive feature – she's a wage-earner round at the Ropeworks."

Tam Gorton scowled.

"With what Torrie pays me and my commission from sales there'll be no need for Jean to work. What decent man would send his wife out to work? Fair affronted Ah am that ye would even think that."

"Apart from that Ah just can't imagine how ye met yer sainted bride-to-be in the first place. If she's that good-living it's not as if she drinks and ye don't go to the kirk. Good God, she must have been cold-sober when she accepted ye!"

"Ye're mibbe not as bright as ye think ye are. Ye ken Torrie lets me sell the bits and pieces he brings down from the Hielans? Jean's been buying knick-knacks fairly regularly and we got chattin. Ah made sure she got some good bargains ..."

Etta threw her shawl round her shoulders.

"Good bargains ye say? Ah just hope Jean Jackson thinks she's got a good bargain with ye. Ye're welcome to each other."

With that Etta stormed out.

FOURTEEN

The years moved on and with each traditional Hogmanay celebration Etta was at a loss to understand where the departing year had gone. The only event which marked off each year for her and Torrie was the now inevitable annual miscarriage. With it came the dark depression and the complaint from 'Dreary' Duncan: "At this rate I'll never be a grandmother. I'll be in my dotage before I have a grandchild of my own to dandle on my poor rheumatic knees."

While to date Etta had been unable, for whatever reason, to bring a healthy, live baby to full term the same could not be said of her hated step-mother. The former Jean Jackson, now the respectable Mistress Tam Gorton had produced three male children to add to Tam's brood and was even now expecting a fourth to pack into the overcrowded flat.

Etta was well aware that what was really gnawing at her was the contrast between Torrie and her father. The latter for all his years was obviously still 'doing it' while her own Torrie, who might reasonably have been expected to be in the full flower of his manhood, had, of late, seemingly given up on the whole idea. Apart from an almost routine, duty coupling as they tried yet again for a child to cement their union there was no intimacy.

Often Etta found herself wondering if it was true as a heavily child-burdened friend had once whispered: "There's nothing much in it for women." From this remembered statement of so-called wedded bliss, Etta would give free rein to the thoughts, the scandalous thoughts, of what her life might have been like had she been, not the discontented wife of Torrie, but rather the bride of Bert Nairn.

Torrie and Bert were due to set off on one of their many trips north to replenish the now dwindling stocks in the carter's yard.

"Yes," Torrie said, "Employing yer father to market our goods was the best move Ah ever made. Even if it does mean more frequent trips for Bert and me to the Hielans."

Etta stared long and hard at her husband. "As long as ye're sure ma father is doin the right thing by ye ... and not skinning off ower much o the profit for himself."

Torrie waved away her words with an impatient gesture. "Ye're still beating away at that old drum?"

When Etta's only reply was a tightening of the lips Torrie went on: "Listen and listen well, for Ah'm saying this for the last time. As long as

Bert and me are making a good living, there's still enough in the pot to let Tam have a wee bit extra profit as well."

Etta in a rare gesture of genuine affection leant forward and grasped her husband's hand.

"Och, Torrie! Ye're a good man. Let's face it, there's no ower many folk would be big-hearted enough to turn a blind eye to my father's thievin ways."

Torrie fixed her with a steely gaze and snatched back his hand. "Aye, Etta. But while we're on the subject it seems to me that ye could be doing with a wee drop more of the milk of human kindness. After all, yer poor father needs all the bawbees he can lay hands on in a house bursting at the seams with hungry weans. And the word on the street is that his not so bonnie Jean is expecting another bairn."

Etta, ever more and more painfully aware of her own barren state, chose to ignore this news of her hated stepmother's latest forthcoming happy event. Hoping to turn the conversation to happier topics she said: "Now then, Torrie ... Ah've been thinking since ye and Bert are planning to set out bright and early tomorrow, how would it be if Ah cooked us an extra tasty supper? Like a wee farewell do."

Far from being delighted at this wifely considerate proposal, Torrie seemed embarrassed. He scratched his head and examined his fingernails before he said: "Aye, it's a good enough idea ... but ... the thing is, for all we make him really welcome each time he comes here, it seems that Bert is getting more reluctant to visit us. Maybe he just feels like the odd man out, him not having a wife or a woman of his own. Anyway, after the last couple of refusals ... we'd maybe best leave well enough alone for a wee while."

Gulping back her disappointment that despite her scheming she would not after all be seeing Bert – the man whose handsome face haunted her every moment – before he left.

Aye, Torrie ye might not know the reason, Etta thought. *But Ah ken exactly why poor Bert will at all costs steer clear o our Duncan household. It's that damned old mother-in-law o mine. She went out o her way on his last visit to make Bert feel really uncomfortable. It was as if the old witch sensed an unseen, unvoiced but very real mystical connection between Bert and me. She watched his and ma every move. Not to mention all her comments about the sanctity of marriage, and how her son was such a wonderful provider although sadly not yet a father.*

So, on that last evening before their departure Etta found herself sharing a rather fraught supper with her sour-faced mother-in-law.

For about the tenth time in as many minutes old Mrs Duncan moaned: "I suppose it's all to your blame that Hector isn't sharing the family meal with us."

Mrs Duncan waved Etta's protests aside.

"No need to play the innocent with me. I could hear the pair of you having a bitter argument before he went out, banging the door behind him. Just what was that all about?"

"Nothin for ye to worry yer old head about, Mother-in-law. Torrie's away down to the Ferry Inn to meet up with Bert and we'll sort out our differences when he gets home before he sets out for the Hielans."

"I do wish you'd stop calling him by that common name, His name is Hector as I've often reminded you before."

It was well into the small hours of the morning before an inebriated Torrie arrived back in Etta's bed and when a sleepy Etta turned to confront him she was met with an avalanche of snoring. Next morning up at the crack of dawn to send him on his way well fed, Etta looked in dismay at her hung-over husband.

"So much for our fond farewell, Torrie."

A bleery-eyed Torrie peered at her. "Don't start on me again, Etta. Ah've business to see to today. Ah've arranged to meet Bert at the quay for an early ferry."

Etta scowled. "Business, bloody business ... it's all ye ever think about. What about me? Och to hell. Get out o my sight. Do yer damned business and don't bother comin back. Ah'm sick o ye. Sick o ye, do ye hear?"

FIFTEEN

With Torrie off on his latest trip, as usual the house seemed strangely quiet without him. Mrs Duncan, as was normal in his absence, grew more demanding day by day.

Scarcely a day passed without Torrie's mother whining: "Is there no sign of my Hector back yet?"

And Etta's constant reply of: "They should be here any day now ... the very minute they have done enough business to keep the wolf from the door for at least another wee while."

Today, however, more than a month since the pair left, Etta felt that her mother-in-law's plaint had a note of genuine concern and, for once, putting aside her usual antipathy to the old woman felt a stab of pity.

"Ah can't think why ye're getting yersel in such a stooshie about this particular trip. It's just Torrrie's regular journey."

Mrs Duncan looked up. "But, Etta."

"But Etta nothing. What ye need right now is a nice hot cup o tea and maybe one o the treacle scones Ah made earlier this morning."

Sitting facing each other on either side of the sitting room fire, Etta still making a determined effort to be pleasant to her despised mother-in-law, smiled.

"There now, is that not better? Tea and sympathy, ye can't beat it, works every time. Ah'm Ah no right?"

Mrs Duncan, widow of ship's captain, who considered herself to be something of 'a gentlewoman in reduced circumstances' and certainly much higher up the social scale than her son's wife, sipped at her tea.

"If I'm being honest, the tea is somewhat stewed for my taste."

Keeping a firm hold on her temper and even tighter grip on her mug of tea lest she pour its contents over the head of the cantankerous old woman, Etta smiled grimly and said: "Leaving aside the question of the tea, stewed or otherwise, surely at least we've managed to settle one thing."

"And what, pray, might that be?"

"Well it's not for want of telling ye now is it? But Ah'm sure that Torrie and Bert will both be fine. There's nothing at all for ye to worry about."

"I just wish I could be as certain as you. In this bad weather those overcrowded cattle ferries are not always safe. Apart from all that ... I've been having some very strange dreams in his absence ..." Mrs Duncan paused and gave Etta a strange, almost gloating look. "If, God forbid, my

Hector did pass from this life before me ... I have determined that you and I would not, could not, possibly go on living here together. This is, after all, my house, left to me by my dear departed husband, God rest his soul. My house and what I say goes!"

Etta stared wide-eyed, dumbstruck for a moment, at her venomous mother-in-law before she rose and towering over the old woman said: "The day that Torrie is no longer with us Ah'll be out that door and as far away from yer moans and groans and yer high-falutin ideas quicker than ye'll get the chance to throw me out. Right, now we both ken where we stand."

"How dare you? I'll not be spoken to in that manner in my own house –."

Anything further was drowned out by a frantic rapping on the brass lion's head door knocker. The staccato tattoo continued to echo along the front hall as Etta made her way to answer the summons.

Secretly glad of the diversion she called back: "It's probably just some excited weans looking for their Hallowe'en and desperate to do their party pieces for us."

They'll be lucky, she thought, *There's damn all enjoyment do be had in this house – far less dookin for apples or jumpin about to catch a bite o a treacle scone.*

When she opened the door, with something of a theatrical gesture, to welcome the expected throng of children the words of welcome and encouragement froze on her lips. She took a step back in surprise. "Oh! It's ye!"

"Aye, Etta Duncan, it's me. Ye look as though ye've seen a ghost."

Etta gave a nervous laugh. "Well, Bert, that's exactly what Ah was expecting – a wheen o Hallowe'en guisers, ghosties, and ghouls."

There was no answering smile from her husband's business partner.

"Can Ah come in for a minute?"

"Of course, come in. Need ye ask? Is Torrie still round at the yard. Sent ye on ahead did he? Wanted to make sure the kettle's on the hob?"

Bert said nothing but followed Etta through the hall to the sitting room where Mrs Duncan sat by the fireside.

"Good evening to ye, Mrs Duncan. Ah'm glad ye're here. What Ah have to say concerns both of ye."

Seated in the master's chair, Bert shifted as if uncomfortable, coughed, and cleared his throat noisily.

"Ah'm truly sorry, ladies, but ... well ... there's no other way to say this ... but it's bad news Ah bring ye ... in fact the worst possible news."

The two women exchanged glances then Mrs Duncan put a trembling hand to her forehead.

"Ah told ye so, Etta! Didn't Ah? Ah told ye something was not right about this trip. My poor Hector has been injured, hasn't he?"

Bert looked down and sat twisting his bonnet in his hands.

"Tell us!" Etta almost screamed at him her nerves shredded by her mother-in-law's babbling recriminations and the suspense.

Still refusing to look at the two women, Bert finally ground out: "There's no easy way to tell ye or lighten yer burden in any measure. Torrie's dead. A hero's death but ... oh, My God ... a dreadful end ... God rest his soul. A hellish end, no other word for it."

There was a stunned silence then Mrs Duncan gave out a banshee-like wail and fell forward in her chair in a faint. Etta leapt from her own chair to stop Mrs Duncan tumbling out of the chair altogether. Having pushed the old lady back into a safer position Etta glanced at Bert. He was slumped in his chair, his head in his hands.

Etta had never seen a grown man cry and, while the sight appalled her, she watched in fascinated horror unable to take her gaze away from this broken man.

Torrie's dead! Why? What happened? A hero's death ... what in God's name can that mean? No, Bert, Ah'm sorry but ye're goin to have to tell us more than the bald fact that my man's dead.

Etta shook herself. *Tea! Ah'll make some tea ... and lace it with a drop or two of the water o life from the medicinal bottle.*

Armed with the fortified tea Etta re-entered the sitting room to find Bert still huddled in the master's chair and Mrs Duncan sitting upright weeping. Forcing a cup and saucer on each of them, she poured the tea then sat down.

"Now, Bert, ye can't leave us hangin like this. Ye've said Torrie died a hero's death. Ah think we've the right to know exactly what happened."

Bert sighed. "It all started out with a mistake on our part. We always tried to be a step or two ahead of the Clearance men – to be well away from any clachan they were working. But that damned day we'd just got to this village and the Factor's men were there. They were trying to throw out an old man – bedridden he was – and he wouldn't let them part him from an old blanket chest. He said it had belonged to his mother as a bride. We could hear the shouting from the yard. That was when the trouble really started ..."

Etta waited more or less patiently as Bert sipped his tea, but when he stared into space and showed no sign of continuing she prompted: "That was when the trouble started ... go on, Bert."

"Aye, Ah can see it yet. They were dragging that poor old man out by the legs with him holding onto the battered old chest as if his very life depended on it and dragging the kist out behind him. The wreckers laughed, kicked the old man's hands 'til he let go and heaved the kist back into the croft they had set fire to. The old man somehow staggered to his feet and back into the building. Quick as a flash Torrie was after him. We could see the kist just in the door. Torrie pushed it back out to get at the crofter who was on his knees trying to push it. As Torrie bent over, a beam hit him on the head and the burning thatch fell on both of them."

Bert shook his head and for a moment Etta thought he was going to start weeping again.

They sat in a silence broken only by Mrs Duncan's weeping.

"Those wreckers stood laughing and joking and wouldn't let anyone near the burning croft until it was just a smouldering ruin."

The remainder of that evening passed in a blur of disbelief at the harsh reality of how one's life can change in an instant.

When Bert finally took his leave standing in the hall at the front door he said to Etta: "Ye might think me a sentimental fool, but when the Factor's men left and Ah found that battered old kist lying where they had left it just beside the door and hardly scorched at all, Ah picked it up and brought it back with me. After all, in one sense, Torrie gave his life for it. It's only fit for firewood really but Ah thought ye might want it as a keepsake ... ye won't have the comfort of a decent burial service or even a proper graveside to visit and mourn."

"That was thoughtful of ye, Bert. But thank ye for leavin it round at the yard for the minute – Ah don't think Ah could bear to look at it yet a while."

Bert nodded. "Of course, Etta, that's as it should be. Ah wouldn't expect less from a grieving widow. But once ye're feeling stronger, ye and Ah will meet at the yard to discuss what's to happen to the business now."

At Bert's words it struck Etta: *That's it, it's true. Ah'm now a widow. There'll be decisions to make in the days to come – not least of which is to think of what Mrs Duncan said about throwing me out if Torrie was dead.*

SIXTEEN

True to her earlier declaration of intent Mrs Duncan soon made it perfectly clear that Etta's days in the family home were numbered. Her campaign started early with snide, hurtful comments, constant criticism of Etta's every move, and spells of most difficult behaviour when Etta tried to reason with her. The trump card a week later came in the form of a robust, obsequious woman, Williamina, supposedly a distant cousin, who arrived unheralded from nearby Port Glasgow.

This crawler calmly announced: "I'm moving in. I'll live here and be a comfort to my poor cousin in her old age. I'll help her try to get over the death of her beloved son, Hector."

Etta simply stared at the apparition in silence.

"When my dear cousin told me that you would soon be leaving, I at once thought it was the least I could do. It would be a sin and against all human decency to leave her to cope with her grief alone and untended."

"Well, good luck to ye. Whoever, ye are. If ye're to be the constant carer and soul mate o old Mrs Duncan ye'll need all the luck, patience, and fortitude ye can lay hands on. Take it from me, Ah speak with the voice o experience."

Still upset from her encounter with Mrs Duncan's cousin Etta went to the yard to meet Bert to discuss business matters and found Bert himself upset.

"The thing is, Etta, Torrie was the brains of the enterprise. Ah was only the interpreter ... After the atrocities Ah've seen in these Highland Clearances ..." Bert's voice broke with emotion. "Ah don't think ever again in this life will Ah set foot back in the Highlands."

At a loss how to deal with a man so obviously showing his emotions Etta simply said: "Bert, why don't ye set about winding up the business and we'll meet to share out the proceeds between us. Ah think that would be best."

Several days later Etta was back in the yard to find Bert in a much happier frame of mind.

"Good morning, Etta. A grand crisp day is it not?"

"It's well seen bein yer own boss suits ye fine. Believe me Ah'm really happy to find ye in such good trim."

"Much of that happy state is down to ye. Between ye sharing what Ah got from the sale of that good stuff in Glasgow and letting me buy the yard and the flat above at a good price ..."

Etta held out a hand to stem the flow.

"Not a word more, Bert. Everything was partly yours anyway after all the help ye gave Torrie. Anyway, Ah should be thankin ye. Now that ye're rentin out the yard as workshop spaces to joiners, carpenters, plumbers and the like, out of the goodness of yer heart, ye've let my father stay on in the flat as yer caretaker for free and even given him a small wage. At least him and his brood o weans will not go homeless and need to join the trek, like so many others, to the dreaded workhouse."

"Ah've got the accounting here for ye, Etta, all properly set out. Ah estimated what we'd be likely to get for what's left in the yard – remember we were pretty well down before Torrie and Ah went off on our last trip. The money's yours as Torrie's widow and ye can collect anytime, either yourself or Ah'll bring it to ye."

"Why, where is it now, Bert?"

"Torrie and Ah opened accounts with a bank in Glasgow. It made it easier working with some of the dealers we sold our stuff to. Here's yer book. Ah had it changed to yer name."

Etta stared in astonishment at the document Bert handed to her."

"Eighteen pounds, Bert? It's a fortune. At the Ropeworks Ah slaved six days a week for four shillings a week and glad to get it. Ye and Torrie must have been making money hand over fist."

"Aye, we didn't do too badly while it lasted. But Torrie wasn't mean with ye, was he?"

"No, Ah'm better dressed now than Ah ever was. Torrie liked to see me smart. And he wasn't tight about money for the housekeeping, although he gave that to his mother and she doled it out."

The two friends went on chatting companionably for a few minutes and at one point Etta was on the point of telling Bert of her own predicament and potential state of homelessness. What held her back was the nagging thought: *Ah've never played the pathetic, helpless woman to any man and Ah'm not about to change my ways now. With this money Torrie left me Ah'll be fine for a spell. Somethin will surely turn up and as usual Ah'll get by under my own steam.*

With a start she realised Bert was speaking to her. "What was that, Bert?"

"Miles away, ye were. Ah was only asking what ye thought of that old kist when the carter finally brought it round to ye last week?"

"A bonnie lookin object, Ah don't think! It really grieves me to think that my Torrie and the old man died on account of that useless piece of junk – neither use nor ornament. A kistful o nothing. Wait, Ah tell a lie. It did contain what looked like a faded bit o curtain material – his mother's wedding veil, do ye think? Ye'll never guess what else was in the kist."

"Go on surprise me. Was it the old man's nightshirt and tassle-toorie or maybe his clay pipe?"

Entering into the joke Etta grinned at him

"Nothin so valuable to him or even so ordinary to the likes o us – Bert, Ah was astonished, it was a winding sheet!'

"Phew! A winding sheet. Ye're right, Etta, it is hard to believe. But it explains why the old man was so desperate to hang onto his kist. It's an old Highland custom that ye keep yer winding sheet handy at all times. Poor old bugger! He needed his winding sheet."

"Well, in the end it didn't do him much as a halfpenny worth o good did it? And it was the death of my good man Torrie."

They stood in silence for a few minutes before Etta said: "Ah'd best be off. Ah can't stand about all day bletherin. Things to do."

"Aye, Etta, no rest for the wicked."

As Etta made to leave,Bert placed a hand on her arm.

"Remember, Etta, any help ye're needing,either ye or Torrie's mother, ye only have to ask and Ah'm yer man. Ah can turn my hand to most things. So any wee job about the house that's needing done, just say the word."

"That's real good o ye. Same old story, isn't it? It's at times like these ye realise who yer real friends are. The fair-weather hangers-on have all long since departed."

SEVENTEEN

Etta arrived at the Duncan house to find Mrs Duncan and her cousin Williamina comfortably ensconced on either side of the sitting room fire.

"This is a lovely cup of tea, Wilma. Just exactly the way I like it."

Wilma simpered at the compliment.

Mrs Duncan placed her cup and saucer on the small table in front of her and turned to Etta.

"I'd offer you a cup, Etta, but you have rather more important matters to deal with than a cup of afternoon tea. As you know, Wilma has been occupying the servant's room in the attic since she arrived. I think it is time you gave up the best front room you and Hector used and let Wilma have it. After all, she is to be my live-in companion. When you leave we'll hire a girl for the rough work as I can't possibly expect Wilma to perform that sort of function."

From Torrie Etta knew that his mother owned her house and lived on an annuity of about two hundred pounds a year making her not wealthy but certainly comfortable by the standards of the time. With that income she should be well able to afford a maid plus possibly a girl for the rough work. Yet Etta had been expected to do everything.

Etta felt her face flush brighter and brighter.

"But it was fine for me, yer son's wife, to be the scodgie?"

Mrs Duncan shrugged. "It was quite fitting. It is what you were brought up to."

Unwilling to let Mrs Duncan or Wilma see how hurt she was Etta turned to leave.

"A moment, Etta," Mrs Duncan said. "Wilma, from the goodness of her heart, and under my direction of course, has shifted some of your bits-and-pieces out to that shed at the end of the garden."

"The shed? The shed! Dear God in heaven ye're expecting me, yer son's recently bereaved widow, to up-sticks and go and live like some tramp in a mouldy old hut at the bottom of yer garden?"

"Of course I do not mean for you to *sleep* in the shed. There simply would not be sufficient room for your belongings in the attic room – which you may occupy until I find a suitable girl to replace you. I assume that by now your father will have offered you shelter and you'll be moving in with him any day now."

"Oh, indeed. So that's yer solution. Let me tell ye, ye interfering old bitch, my domestic arrangements are my business."

"Really, Etta, I can't think why you are making such a fuss. We talked about this long ago. Now all that has happened is that some of your effects have been stored for you – including, I may say that battered old chest that's been cluttering up the best bedroom ever since Bert's carters brought it round here."

"That battered old kist is a sacred memorial to Torrie's memory –"

"Sacred memorial, stuff and nonsense! I shall remember my dear son, Hector in a fitting manner. I'll have nothing whatever to do with that pathetic chest. No, Hector shall have a proper grave stone to stand beside the monument to his father, my dear husband, lost at sea these many years ago."

Etta fled from the house to the garden hut to see what items of her belongings had been ejected.

A quick glance at the neatly arranged pile of her worldly goods in the garden shed was all Etta needed to see that Wilma had very efficiently carried out the bidding of her hostess. There, where she could not possibly miss it sat the kist in the middle of the pile. The rejected kist 'fit only for firewood'.

Her temper boiled to the surface as Etta thought of the way life in general, and her mother-in-law in particular, had treated her. She cast about for something, anything, on which she could vent her rage. In the far corner of the hut amongst a collection of abandoned old tools she spotted a sturdy-looking axe. Seizing it she muttered: "Fit only for firewood? Then firewood ye shall damned well have ... and ye can gather it up yersels in yer lily-white, ladylike hands."

Setting to work with a will, each time the axe crashed down on the chest she relived every sarcastic comment, each snide remark, every embarrassment from her mother-in-law from the very day and hour she set foot as 'Hector's below the salt' bride in his 'beloved' mother's home. The lid demolished and the sides splintered and falling away Etta brought her axe down square on the bottom. It split and parted a little in the middle.

A false bottom?

Etta pushed the ruined sides out of her way and moved the two pieces further apart. There was something there! Several small canvass bags. She lifted one out. It was quite heavy and made a clinking sound. Undoing the drawstring she tipped some of the contents onto her hand. Sovereigns! Gold sovereigns, golden guineas. Etta lost count at sixty and there were still some coins in the bag. No wonder the old man had tried to fight for the kist. Packed tight in the small space of the false bottom wrapped in the canvass bags the coins had made no sound or given any indication of their presence.

Scrabbling in the ruins of the chest Etta found six of the canvass bags Each full of coins. How had a poor old crofter come by this fortune? Etta searched her memory for any details Bert had told them about the clachan and its inhabitants. No one had claimed the old man's body, or what was left of it after the fire, or shown any interest in the chest. Bert had even had to pay for help to bury both the old man and Torrie. The locals had told Bert the man hadn't lived there all his life. He'd been at sea or abroad and returned to take the croft when his parents died and made no attempt to mingle or renew acquaintance with others from his youth. So, no one had any claim to the money, however it had been obtained. It was Etta's

"Ah didn't ken there was this much money in the whole o Greenock."

She put a trembling hand to her brow. "Oh praise be ... Ah'm rich! Me, Etta Gorton, the widow-woman Duncan. God help us, Ah'm rich ... Ah'm bloody rich!"

Etta straightened up and took a step back and in doing so knocked a china chamber pot off the shelf where it had been precariously balanced. To Etta, the pot seemed to fall in slow motion before it hit the floor and smashed into dozens of pieces and she made no attempt to catch it.

There was a time when letting such a chamber pot fall and break – especially one not belongin to me – would have been the end o the world. They cost a pretty penny ... but now? Ah'm rich. Ah could buy a whole manufactory o damned chanties ... and not notice the dent in my purse.

At this thought, Etta collapsed in hysterical laughter and when that finally abated came the sobering realisation that at last, long last, she was what she had always wanted to be – a free woman, not beholden to any man, woman, or child. Her mother-in-law had publicly declared she wanted nothing to do with Etta or the kist, and Bert had also disclaimed any interest in the kist, so the money was all hers.

Taking off the shawl which she was still wearing from her trip to the yard, Etta wrapped the seven canvass bags in it then placed the bundle in a coarse potato sack Wilma had left draped over Etta's belongings for her convenience.

With the threat of being evicted from Mrs Duncan's house had first arisen Etta had considered her options. She would not move in with her father and Jean Jackson, even if such accommodation was offered. Taking a menial live-in post with one of the more well-to-do families was a possibility. With her education becoming a live-in companion was probably beyond her reach. Thinking on these lines she had tentatively talked in very general terms with some of the women from the church – not Mrs Duncan's elevated circle – and had learned that there were quite a few 'gentlewomen in reduced circumstances', poorer than Mrs Duncan, who might not be above offering accommodation in exchange for some household duties. This was what Etta had decided to explore, but finding the hoard of coin changed her perspective. She would visit one of these ladies and find if they would take her in as a 'paying guest'.

Having thus decided on her plan of action with a much lighter heart and a spring in her step, she left the shed and re-entered the house to confront her mother-in-law and Wilma.

They stopped in mid-sentence as Etta walked in. Forcing what she hoped was a sugar-sweet smile Etta said: "Ah really must thank ye for taking the trouble to move my stuff. It was really kind o ye."

Etta almost burst out laughing at the thought of her wonderful secret and Mrs Duncan and Wilma stared at her. She coughed and continued: "Ah'm really tongue-tied by yer thoughtfulness ... but what Ah'm trying to say is, thanks for yer effort, it's been a really big help."

Mrs Duncan's frown clearly indicated this was not the response she had been expecting but Etta didn't give her time to speak.

"With yer help it means Ah'll be able to leave yer house much quicker than Ah expected – within the next couple o days Ah think."

"But where will you go at such short notice?" Mrs Duncan said. "You already said your father's flat is already too crowded. Also, you must not forget as a respectable widow-woman and one bearing the respected name of Duncan you will obviously have to maintain a certain standard of morals and decorum."

"Ye might have considered that before ye decided to have me leave yer home. But don't concern yerself Mother-in-law Ah will find a place fitting for my Torrie's widow."

With that Etta swept out of the room and upstairs to the attic there to unpick the hems of her skirts and sew in some of her coins.

In two days Etta had found room and board with one of the 'gentlewomen in reduced circumstances' and moved in. Her hostess delighted with the golden guinea advance payment couldn't be more affable and accommodating.

Greatly daring, Etta travelled to Glasgow by train, first class, to visit the bank holding her eighteen pounds inherited from Torrie. The manager at first merely formal with the widow of a past client became positively obsequious when Etta instead of withdrawing her money as he obviously expected, set down on his desk two canvass bags of sovereigns for deposit to her account.

When waiting in the station for her return to Greenock Etta saw posters advertising free land in Canada for able-bodied men willing to go there and work the land. On the hour's journey she thought about this.

Men again! It's always the same, they get free land just for going there. What about free land for a woman. Not a chance in hell.

However, the poster had given her the glimmering of an idea and next day she set out to find Bert Nairn.

When she asked him about the posters and the free land he said: "Aye, there's many a crofter evicted in the Clearances that would jump at the chance. But they've got to get there first. It's five pounds for a steerage ticket from Gourock to Quebec. Even if they can scrape that up without starving the family, they'd need something to live on when they get there and to travel to their land."

"Is the five pounds just for the man?"

"There's the rub. How long would he have to slave in Canada to scrape up the five pounds for his wife and half that for each child over one and under fourteen? Why are ye asking, Etta?"

She shook her head. "Just curious. Ah know ye help out some of the crofters when ye can. Have ye never thought of going to Canada yourself?"

"Not now. Thanks first to Torrie, and now to ye, Ah've got a nice little carter's business and the rent for space in the yard. Oh, ye'll need to excuse me, there's a man Ah have to talk to. MacKay, fresh down from Sutherland, my own area, poor soul, a hard working crofter with six of a family thrown out with only the clothes they stood up in."

Etta watched as Bert walked over to man.

MacKay was a well built, fresh-faced man not yet showing the pallid face and drawn expression of those dispossessed who had been in Greenock for months, destitute and starving. Obviously he was asking Bert about work and when Bert said he had nothing and offered MacKay some money it was angrily refused.

On impulse Etta followed MacKay when he left the yard and caught up with him further down the street.

"Mr MacKay, can we talk?"

"Mistress Duncan?"

"Ye know me?"

"Ah've seen ye talk with Bert Nairn. He said ye were his partner's widow."

"Have ye seen the billboards about free land in Canada?"

"Aye, a nice dream, but a man has to get there first."

"Suppose Ah had a way to get ye and yer family there. Would ye be interested?"

"Ah'll not accept charity." MacKay made to turn and walk away.

"Just hold on a minute, man. Ah'm not offerin charity. Ye'd be earnin yer way. Is there someplace we could sit down and talk."

"Nairn helped us get a place to put down our heads, but it's no place for a lady like yourself."

Etta looked at MacKay and burst out laughing.

MacKay's face reddened, and again he started to walk away.

Etta managed to control herself. "Please, Mr MacKay, Ah not laughin at ye, honest. Ah've not often been taken for a lady. Don't let this fancy dress fool ye. Ah was brought up in Mince Collop Lane."

MacKay grinned. "Aye, Ah've seen it, but it's a palace compared to where we are ... but all right. Mrs MacKay will be black affronted, she aye kept a neat croft."

The outhouse the MacKay's were living in, in a corner of builder's yard, was swept as clean as Mrs Mackay could make it. She was indeed flustered and annoyed at her husband for bringing a lady there, but bustled to stoke up the small potbellied stove with scraps of wood and offered tea.

Etta almost refused then realised that refusal would give offence.

Finally, seated on small tea chests Etta was able to broach the subject.

"Ah was talking to yer husband about the free land in Canada that a man can get just by claiming it."

Mrs MacKay nodded warily.

"The problem is it's only men that can claim it ..."

"Aye, 'tis ever so," Mrs MacKay said.

"What would ye think if Ah was to pay yer fares, steerage, for all of ye, to Canada. In return ye would sign the land over to me and work it as a tenant farmer?"

"We'd need money to set up –"

"Ah'd see to that."

Mr and Mrs MacKay looked at each other.

"What would there be to stop me – once ye've paid yer good money for our fares – when we got to Canada just taking off for the wilds with our claim to the land and never repaying ye as much as a brass farthing?"

"Yer word as a Highlander. If we shake on it, that is yer bond."

"No offence meant, Mrs Duncan, but if ye have title to the land what would there be to stop ye evicting us – as his lordship did in Sutherland – and leaving us even worse off in a foreign land?"

"No offence taken. Ah've talked to a lawyer about that. Once ye get title in Canada, before ye sign it over to me, we can have an agreement drawn up that gives ye life tenancy, and yer children after ye the right to buy the land at the fair market value at the time. The lawyer Ah spoke to here gave me the name o one he has dealt with in Canada."

They sat in silence for a short time before MacKay stood and held out his hand.

"A deal, Mrs Duncan?"

"A deal, Mr Mackay," Etta said and shook his hand.

MacKay cleared his throat.

"I hope ye won't think me too forward, Mrs Duncan ... but would ye consider doing the same for my cousin Hamish and his bride? Ah can vouch for the fact that Hamish is a good worker."

That would give me two plots o land, probably side by side and two tenant farmers. Ah could afford that and I'd get some income from them after they settled.

"Yes, Mr MacKay, Ah'll do that."

The more Etta thought about it the better an idea it seemed and within the week she had a total of four immigrant families signed up to her plan. The one proviso she put on them was that they were not to tell anyone else in Greenock about it – not even Bert Nairn.

The agreements reached, Etta booked passage for all of them – cabin class for herself and steerage for the families – to sail in just under a month. Actually parting with the money for the voyage gave Etta a momentary twinge it was more money than she'd ever spent in her whole life, but relaxed thinking it barely made a dent in her fortune.

EIGHTEEN

With business matters attended to Etta felt a rising tide of joy and expectation as she prepared to leave forever her old life in Scotland.

She told no-one of her plans although she had fleetingly thought of telling her father. However, his words when she told him she would have to leave Mrs Duncan's home came flooding back.

"Just as long as ye're no lookin for bed and board in my flat when Mother-in-law Duncan chucks ye out, ye can go wherever the hell ye like. Ye're a grown woman now and no longer my responsibility."

Ah never was yer wee girl, father, Etta thought. *Ye had me out slavin at the Ropeworks when Ah was still but a bairn. Workin my fingers to the bone for yer drink money.*

As she bustled about with her preparations Etta mentally thanked old Mrs Duncan for all that she had inadvertently taught her. Not for nothing had Etta minutely observed the manners, clothes, and speech patterns of her mother-in-law, that self-declared 'gentlewoman in reduced circumstances'. Etta was bright and a quick learner. She knew her table manners and the correct use of cutlery, and while her social skills might seem to some 'countrified' she was sure she could 'pass'.

Her hostess since she left the Duncan household turned out to have been a teacher in her past. When Etta showed a willingness to learn the old instructor in her landlady came to the fore and proceeded to improve Etta's speech and grammar.

While Torrie had not been stingy about dressing her, Etta felt that his mother had deliberately tried to keep her 'dressed down' to suit her station as subservient to her mother-in-law. So while her clothes were certainly respectable – far beyond anything she had been able to afford before she married Torrie – they were not in the least fashionable. This Etta remedied as she waited for her sailing date.

On the appointed day Etta had the fleeting thought: *I just wish my father, his bonnie Jean, Mrs Duncan, Bert and maybe even some of my old workmates from the Ropeworks could see me in all my finery. They'd have a fit!*

However, Etta had decided to cut all ties. Quite deliberately, although she had told Bert she was going to Canada, she had not told him the exact date.

The last thing I would need is an emotional farewell, complete with a kilted piper on the quayside. No, from now on my links with Scotland are well and truly cut.

The Gortons of Greenock

Determined to make the right impression from the word go Etta had decided on one final flourish. With that in mind she had treated herself to the entirely needless luxury of arriving at the quayside in a hired hackney, her luggage having already been delivered to the ship by carter,

So, as she stepped down from the carriage in her new finery one of the ship's officers at once materialised to escort her to the waiting vessel. With an expression on her face to indicate that she was aware of the smell of rotting fish nearby she made her grand entrance.

Glancing at the queue of people lining the dockside she gave her escort a look of enquiry.

"No need for you to worry about them, madam. They're what you might call the lower orders ... steerage passengers all. We don't allow them aboard until the very last minute before we set sail. After all, they might as well get all the fresh air they can before they're battened down for days on end in the hold of the ship."

Etta nodded her head but made no reply. The officer, a few minutes later in handing her off the gangway said: "It's only people of quality, such as yourself, Madam, who have the privilege of joining the ship early."

In that instant Etta knew she had arrived. Had it not been unseemly she would have hugged the young sailor.

Yes! I was right! The extra money on the hackney, the new clothes, the smart luggage ... it was all worth every penny.

For the first time in her life, she, a formerly ragged, downtrodden, underpaid employee of the Greenock Ropeworks, had been classed, on first acquaintance and without a doubt as Quality.

Never again will I allow myself to be a victim. I am my own person, beholden to no man. With the money I already have and the fortune I'm determined to make in Canada, I'll be a force, a strong woman, to be reckoned with.

Ensconced in her cabin Etta looked round in wonder at the lush accommodation and smiled quietly at the thought: *I wonder if I would have been made quite so welcome had I arrived with my hands, not encased in the finest, soft leather gloves but bleeding and red-raw from working at the Ropeworks, my face pinched and blue with cold, and in rags. No, it wouldn't have been a comfortable cabin for me but as a member of the 'great unwashed' I'd now be standing out there on the windswept quayside awaiting permission to board.*

NINETEEN

Seated at the Captain's table with the other handful of people who made up the full complement of cabin passengers and ever conscious of her new station in life Etta was determined not to put a foot wrong. She decided to take time to study her fellow passengers before committing herself to any hastily-engaged-in shipboard friendships.

After all she reasoned, *quite apart from the effort of keeping up appearances as a lady of quality, who knows but that some of these shipboard companions might later feature in some way in my new life in Canada.*

A Mrs Carlisle the only other woman passenger sitting across the table from Etta said: "Am I to understand Mrs Duncan that you are going to Canada to join your husband? It is unusual to see an unaccompanied female on these ships."

Etta realised the woman was fishing for information. She assumed a look which she hoped portrayed deep sorrow and said: "Oh, dear me, no, Mrs Carlisle. I'm afraid you have been sadly misinformed. The truth of the matter is ..." Etta dabbed at her eyes with a dainty lace handkerchief. "Actually, I'm going to Canada to fulfil an ambition of my dear-departed husband."

She allowed Mrs Carlisle and the others to digest this rather cryptic news before she leaned forward and said: "Mrs Carlisle, I beg of you, please don't be embarrassed. You had no way of knowing of the sad circumstances of my journey."

Now that she had the attention of the whole table Etta wondered if she had blundered since she had no idea whatever what her late husband's ambition might be. Playing for time she dabbed again at her eyes.

The bearded Captain met her gaze.

"There now, Mrs Duncan, please don't distress yourself further. I am sure whatever your mission may be, if it is to honour your husband's memory, then it is indeed a worthy cause."

There were nods of assent around the table and Etta felt relieved.

"Thank you, Captain, you are very kind."

Perhaps to bridge the resulting lull in conversation the Captain said: "Mrs Duncan has very graciously paid for extra provisions for the steerage passengers and I understand that some of her former tenants are aboard and on their way to a new life in Canada."

There were nods of approval and Etta felt that her status had just gone up in the social scale without any effort on her part.

The Gortons of Greenock

Throughout the remainder of the voyage Etta was treated with a certain reserve as suited her obviously high social standing. Having got the measure of Mrs Carlisle, Etta then set about making a confidante of her, feeding her such snippets of information as she wished the gossipy woman to pass on to the other passengers.

Thus by the end of the voyage it was common knowledge among passengers and crew that Mrs Duncan was ... "A wealthy widow whose late husband – very big in the import trade, you know – had wished her – since they were childless, you know – to help those poor souls displaced by the Highland Clearances."

How this version was reconciled with the Captain's 'former tenants', Etta neither knew nor cared

Etta's arrival in Canada was almost a mirror image of how she had joined the ship. Having said her farewells to her fellow passengers she was graciously escorted to the dockside all the time aware of the pale, pitiful souls on all sides. These, she realised, were the immigrants now released from the steerage holds.

65

TWENTY

By the end of her first month in the land of opportunity Etta had come to the conclusion that Canada was not for her after all. Previously unseen difficulties and legal complexities regarding the transfer of Government land to a woman on her own arose and it was soon apparent that as a single woman, widow or not, without the customary, conventional, legally wed husband at her side matters were going to be difficult.

This, of course, meant that to keep close to the families in whom she had invested money for their fares she would have to join them in the hazardous journey by covered wagon west to where land was available. Although Etta knew she was capable of being as tough and fearless as any other intrepid pioneer, she was loath go give up her hard-earned position in the eyes of the world as a lady of quality.

Having made up her mind, Etta arranged a meeting with the MacKays and the other families involved in her scheme to tell them of her decision to return to Scotland.

Following her announcement there was a long silence before Mr MacKay spoke on behalf of all: "But Mistress Duncan, what about the deal we made with ye? If ye see problems in getting legal title to land and ye are not now coming with us, how will we ever be able to repay you for the money ye put up in good faith for our boat fares? Surely ye must see that will put us all in a very difficult position."

"I want no return on that so-called investment. You are none of you beholden to me in any way whatsoever. You are not my slaves. You are free to make a decent living for yourselves – but it is a pioneering life in which I want no part."

Mr MacKay looked round the others. "Ah am sure such a gesture is very noble, Mistress Duncan, but as Ah have made clear to ye from day one – and Ah am sure Ah speak for all – Ah will not accept charity. Ye must come west with us, stay with my family, at least until we can scrape enough money together to repay ye."

"Mr MacKay, Sir, I appreciate what you are saying, but as a free woman I allow no man to dictate to me. I do *not have to do* anything other than what I choose to do. My mind is made up. I have chosen to return to Scotland and I shall be sailing at the first opportunity."

"But Ah still do not understand why you would do this for us."

Etta smoothed down her gloves giving herself time to reply.

"I am doing this in memory of my dear departed husband, Torrie, and an old Highland gentleman whose name I shall never know. Both of them lost their lives in the Hell of the Highland Clearances."

Mr MacKay mumbled: "Is there nothing we can do?"

Etta nodded. "Yes, make the most of your opportunities here in Canada. Who knows but that you can help some other immigrants not as fortunate as yourselves. Keep alive the horrendous story of the Clearances. Now I'm sorry I don't have the Gaelic but in parting I wish you all, good health, and every good blessing to you.

If Etta had been as a lady of quality on her outward voyage to Canada that was as nothing compared to her treatment on her return journey. The fame of the largesse she had distributed to the victims of the Highland Clearances seemed to have gone before her. She was waited on hand and foot. What made the voyage even more pleasant was that not only was the ship's Captain enamoured of her but so also was another handsome passenger, Callum Cunningham.

I am really spoiled for choice, Etta thought. *Talk about shipboard romance. Just as well my days as dutiful little wife to any man are truly over. Still, they are not to know that. No harm in a little flirting. It'll help pass the time – better than being stuck in my cabin doing my embroidery.*

With promises of undying friendship ringing in her ears Etta disembarked immediately the ship docked at Greenock. Before boarding the waiting coach she stared at the quayside bollards on which she had once sat as a desperate, suicidal, rape victim contemplating a watery grave in the Clyde.

She was startled out of her reverie by Craig Cunningham's voice`: `So Mistress Duncan – Etta, if may be so bold – is this you back to old haunts and friends here in Greenock?"

At these words Etta's mind pictured the blood-soaked streets of the Greenock Massacre, her erstwhile friends, and the noise sweat and tears of the Greenock Ropeworks.

Turning to Cunningham she gave him her most gracious smile. "Greenock? No, I cut all ties here when my late husband passed from this life. It holds too many memories for me."

"I'm very glad to hear that, dear lady. I myself have some business to transact here then it's off to Glasgow for me."

"As for me, I cannot yet say where I intend to settle. But, yes, I do have your address. So, who knows we may meet again."

TWENTY ONE

It was the Second City of the Empire that claimed Etta for its own. Having taken a long, discerning look at the vibrant, teeming, but above all friendly city Etta decided: *This is the place for me.*

While Etta freely admitted the well-documented history of the 'Dear Green Place' was interesting enough, what really fascinated her was that, as had been the case in the Greenock of her youth, two very different cultures existed in Glasgow. On one hand there was the ragged army of men, women, and even children who laboured hard in the city's mills, manufactories, and coal mines. Then on the other side of the great social divide, and as far removed from the labouring classes as if from a different planet, were the comfortably situated 'haves'. Well entrenched in the smart set of Glasgow's city life was Callum Cuningham, Etta's shipboard companion and now her persistent would be suitor.

Etta smiled as she recalled the immaculately dressed widower's latest visit to her at her refined lodgings in Park Circus. As always on such occasions the Misses Fraser, her ultra-correct landladies, bowled over by the bouquet-bearing Callum's appearance, manners and charm ushered him in with all due respect for his superior station in life. He was shown into the guest drawing room, guided to the most comfortable chair, then waited on hand and foot throughout the ritual of afternoon tea. No sooner had he left than Dolina and Fanny Fraser were all agog to hear the latest developments in the ongoing saga.

Already growing weary of the trite conversation Etta said: "Again, ladies, I tell you Mr Cunninghan is only a good friend – a kindly and reliable friend, nothing more. Certainly, we met on board a ship, but whatever you may have heard, or perhaps imagined, about shipboard romances conducted under a moonlit sky such a scenario was never once part of my experience."

"But, Mistress Duncan, surely–"

"But nothing, Miss Fraser. Honestly, I do hate to spoil your romantic illusions but the truth of the matter is this – battling across the Atlantic in the gales of mid-winter, any romantic attachment was the furthest thing from my mind, I do assure you."

"But the dear gentleman does seem to be genuinely fond of you. Anyone can see that."

"Well, that's as may be. But having seem me at my worst and kindly escorting me as I tottered around the deck trying to find my sea-legs would, I suppose, have given us a fairly solid basis for a lasting friendship."

The faces of both sisters crumpled in disappointment.

"But, Mistress Duncan, such a fine handsome man, a widower no less, clearly unattached and so well doing in his business would be ideal for you."

"Yes," the other sister added, "The handsome Mr Cunningham would be a grand catch for you."

"I was not aware that I had my net out to catch any man."

"Oh, I'm sure we both know that in your circumstances you have no actual need for a husband to support you. But even so, the pair of you would make a very handsome couple."

Later the same week as Etta strolled towards the Establishment for Genteel Ladies to be in time for high tea she was aware that to the casual observer she must appear to be a 'Lady of Quality' taking the air with not a single care in the world.

However, her mind was far from tranquil. It was alive with ideas, memories. Although she still had enough capital to allow her to live comfortably on the income from it she was not looking forward to a life of total idleness devoid of any meaningful activity. Lost in thought Etta was suddenly aware she had wandered into an area she had not visited before. She reached the top of an incline and turned left into a street parallel to Sauchiehall Street and found herself looking along a row of rather grand-looking terraced houses. At the end of the row there was a sturdy wooden stake bearing a tattered paper sign: *To Let.*

Etta stood surveying the building and thought: *Yes! I can visualise what this tired old building can become with a bit of tender loving care. Right, Etta, my girl let's memorise the details of the factor's agent and get right down to Hope Street first thing on Monday morning.*

Negotiations complete, the missive for the lease duly signed, and with the keys of Rowanbrae clutched in her hands Etta broke the news to her landladies.

"But Mistress Duncan – Etta, my dear – why? Haven't you been happy here with us? With your own suite of rooms – the best in the house as you very well know ..."

Dolina's twin took up the story: "And quite apart from your creature comforts here in our lovely home, the three of us all get on so well together don't we?"

Etta made no comment and Fanny went on: "Then, of course, there is that other matter, on a much more personal level – what on earth is your Mr Cunningham going to make of it?"

With great precision Etta laid her cup and saucer on the little table beside her chair and keeping a firm hold on her temper and the timbre and volume of her voice, said: "Ladies. I thought we had already dealt with all that romantic nonsense. He is not my Mr Cunningham, never has been, and never will be."

Etta thinking to lighten the air a little in the ensuing silence said in a friendly coaxing tone: "Once I am settled in my new home you will, of course, come to visit. Once you've seen me in my very own establishment I am sure you will love Rowanbrae every bit as much as I already do."

There was a united gasp of horror followed by meaningful looks between the sisters before Fanny nervously clearing her throat said: "Etta, my dear, when you said you had taken the lease of a largish house we were worried, concerned enough for you – it was a very big undertaking on your own. But you neglected to tell us the name of the house. If it is indeed Rowanbrae, then that puts an entirely different aspect on the whole project."

Dolina placed a trembling hand on Etta's arm.

"Rowanbrae? That is the name you said? Somewhere behind Sauchiehall Street, up a hill, near Rose Street?"

"Yes, you have it exactly. What's the problem with the name? Rowan trees are lucky."

"Oh, It's not the name we're worried about – pretentious though it is to name a terraced house – it's the house itself ..."

Fanny nodded. "The house has been empty for years. A man murdered his wife there and people say she haunts it."

TWENTY TWO

With the house key firmly in her hand, Etta admitted to herself a feeling of trepidation as she stood on the doorstep of Rowanbrae. Then, squaring her shoulders she thrust the key into the lock and opened the door.

The entrance hall was imposing from the end of which rose a circular, wrought iron staircase. Two reception rooms, a cavernous kitchen and butler's pantry comprised the main floor. On a half landing on the way upstairs, luxury of luxuries, was an indoor water closet and on the first floor were six bedrooms.

As Etta wandered round, opening doors, inspecting cupboards, at the rear of the kitchen much to her surprise one door revealed a narrow staircase. Following it up took her to the first floor corridor, but the staircase went on, leading to two cramped attic rooms.

Of course, Etta thought, *a servant's stair and servant's quarters. Yes, this place will fit my needs perfectly. A spacious suite of rooms, overlooking the front, for myself will leave me four letting rooms. The ideal tenants would be ambitious girls — shop assistants in one of the more up-scale stores. Such girls need decent lodgings and a good address within walking distance of these shops. They couldn't afford the exaggerated charges of such snobbish establishments as the Misses Frasier — even if these ladies would lower themselves to renting rooms to them.*

Three months later, Etta had Rowanbrae finished to her satisfaction. The one-time butler's pantry was now a small bedroom for her cook-housekeeper and a young girl — maid-of-all-work — was established in one of the maid's rooms in the attic.

Now to find suitable tenants.

Etta lost no time in introducing herself to the managers of fashionable lady's outfitters in Sauchiehall Street and Buchanan Street. One, initially somewhat surprised at her mission, looking as she did every bit the lady, he passed her on to the dragoness in charge of the girls. In the early stages of her conversation with this madam, it dawned on Etta what was passing through the Tartar's mind.

She thinks I'm a madam from a high class 'house' looking for girls 'to lead astray'.

Somewhat mollified by Etta's explanation the manageress conceded it was difficult for 'her girls' to find suitable accommodation at reasonable prices and she agreed to visit Etta at Rowanbrae for afternoon tea on her first available afternoon free.

The visit went well and the very next week two girls came to Rowanbrae seeking lodgings. The dragoness had been true to her word and had not only told 'her own girls' about Rowanbrae but had passed on the information to other ladies in charge of assistants in stores along Sauchiehall Street and Buchanan Street.

The two girls sat having supper with Etta in the now elegant dining room at Rowanbrae. Etta had just commented that she felt fortunate in her choice of tenants but the younger of the two, Una Malcolm, smiled.

"No, Mistress Duncan we're the lucky ones."

Madge Sloane nodded. "Yes, indeed. If my granny in Partick could see me now. Dining in state with a grand lady like yourself. A lady of quality, no less."

At this, the most sincere compliment Etta had ever received in her entire life, she felt her eyes fill with tears and she dabbed at both eyes with her lace handkerchief.

"Thank you, Madge for that wonderful compliment ..."

Before she went on, visions of her past life contrasting with the present made Etta laugh uncontrollably, causing the two girls to look at each other in concern.

Etta sat up straighter in her chair. "Sorry about that, girls. The mind plays strange tricks on you. I suddenly thought of a boss I once had, a real slave-driver he was, who far from looking on me as a lady of quality thought I was a lazy, good-for-nothing, slut of a lassie."

A scandalised intake of breath greet this revelation and the girls gazed wide-eyed across the table at their elegant landlady.

"A little explanation is due, I believe." Etta smiled. "I was not always a lady. Whatever socially correct manners, decorum, and, I suppose, mannerisms, I now possess, and use to the full advantage – all of these I learnt. I learnt by trial and error; by watching and copying the conduct, table manners and speech of my so-called betters."

"But, surely, Mistress Duncan – our social betters, ladies of quality are born not made ..."

Madge nodded her agreement of Una's statement. "Yes, we're all taught to know our place. Doesn't that hymn even spell it out for us: 'the rich man in his castle, the poor man at his gate'?"

Etta smiled. "Can't say I've ever paid too much attention to hymns as social primers, but ..."

"But what?" Both girls said.

"I believe that anyone, with a bit of studying, a modicum of common sense, and even only one good quality outfit, plus, of course, correct speech patterns can be a lady. If not a lady to the core then at least sufficiently refined as to put on such a façade as to fool the world at large."

'So, Mistress Duncan," Una said, "if I, or we, follow your lead in table manners and all the rest of that rigmarole, then we could pass ourselves off as ladies as good as any bool-in-the-mooth toff?"

Etta laughed. "Not perhaps the most elegant way of expressing it, but, yes. Anyway, apart from anything else, has it never occurred to either of you to wonder why I so often join with the pair of you in the dining room for Violet's tasty suppers?"

The girls exchanged rather shamefaced glances before Madge said: "Yes, we did wonder about that. Then we decided it must one or other of two things ..."

"Which were?"

"To check that no food was being wasted by our sneaking it out of the dining room to feed starving relatives ... or ... in case we were making off with the family silver ..."

They all laughed at the absurdity of the suggestions.

"Joking aside, girls. There is a difference between looking the part of being a lady, and actually being one. The whole concept of good manners is just another name for kindly consideration of others."

Madge nodded. "I know exactly what you mean about the difference between looking and sounding like a lady and behaving like one. One woman in a swanky emporium where I worked as a very junior sales girl was more royal than all the Royal Family rolled into one. She certainly looked the part. She always gushed over any well-to-do customer but as far as anyone else was concerned ... a nippy sweetie, making everybody's life a misery."

"Aye, Madge," Una burst in, "there's at least half-a-dozen o' those stuck up harridans in every store and apart from treating their staff like slaves you should see them when an ordinary shopper – one not oozing money – comes in. You'd think they were doing them a favour serving them."

Etta sighed. "Well ... that puts my mind at ease. Up 'til now I was labouring under the delusion I had met the only one of the breed ... and I've often felt very guilty about what I'd done. I was somewhat less than kind to her."

"Less than kind?" Una said.

"What on earth had you done to make you feel guilty?" Madge said.

"I demanded to see her entire stock of evening gloves, debated and dawdled over every single pair, then declined them all in my best Lady-of-the-Manor voice and sailed out of the emporium without buying a thing."

The girls looked at each other then burst out laughing.

"Is that it?" Madge said. "That's what you've been feeling guilty about?"

"You can take it from us," Una said, "High Society Ladies do exactly what you've described all the time. Nothing new there. Many a time I've been bawled at by the floorwalker for not being quick enough to clear up the mess some madam left on my counter."

"I suppose when I thought about it later I realised perhaps she was only trying to do exactly what I had done – claw her way up to a higher level of society. Also, perhaps, the difference in the prospective commission between a sale to me and one to a poorly dressed Glasgow body might have something to do with it."

Marge gave a rueful grin. "Now you've got me feeling guilty. If there was a well dressed lady like yourself and a dowdy wee Glasgow wifie waiting to be served, I'd push the junior onto the wee wifie and I'd go for the hope of the bigger commission."

Etta laughed. "Well, all that aside it was that encounter that gave me the idea of starting up this boarding house for girls like yourself. Girls in need of affordable lodgings near the big stores in Sauchiehall Street and Buchanan Street. A place where they might also learn some of the airs and graces to help them advance their station in the world."

TWENTY THREE

The years rolled on and again it was the month of July. The annual 'Fair Fortnight' when everyone with the price of a boat ticket to Dunoon or Rothesay, or even the luxury of the Isle of Arran, fled the City.

For the first time in all the years since she had opened Rowanbrae Etta found herself alone in the house and at something of a loose end. Even Violet, Rowanbrae's chief-cook-and-bottle-washer, had gone off on a visit to her Granny so Etta couldn't even ring for her to serve afternoon tea.

As she wandered round fussily moving ornaments from one location to another she stopped short with a silver candelabra in her hand.

This is ridiculous, Etta thought, *Don't I have any interest other than being the chatelaine of Rowanbrae, looking after my girls and bossing Violet? If all else fails I suppose I could, like all the rest, be off to the Broomielaw and hop on a boat for a sail 'doon the watter'. Heavens above I could well afford it.*

But what would be the point? With everyone else enjoying each others company I'd feel even more miserable trailing around like a lost soul on my own.

Etta sat and brooded for a short time before the thought struck her that she hadn't visited the Fraser sisters, Fanny and Dolina, for over a year. She certainly owed them a visit. She'd been so busy she hadn't had time for social visiting and the twins had been good friends to her when she first came to Glasgow.

Unlike the usual downpour which seemed to be more or less expected, if not gladly accepted, as the norm for the Glasgow Fair Holiday, the sun shown brilliantly as Etta made her way to Park Circus.

Feeling in a much happier frame of mind Etta rapped the lion's head on the brass door. About to knock again Etta was startled when the door was opened, not by the maid, but by Fanny herself who stood staring wordlessly at her.

"Oh, it's you," Fanny said but made no move to admit Etta.

Puzzled and confused Etta started blethering about the unusual weather for the Fair Fortnight and ended with: "So, I just thought I'd drop by and see you folk."

As Etta's words trailed off, Fanny glanced up and down at her summery apparel.

"Well, since you've braved this heatwave to venture out into the near deserted City streets, I suppose you'd best come in."

I've had more gracious invitations, Etta thought, but said aloud: "Thank you, yes. I would appreciate getting in out of this baking heat. We're not used to it, now are we?"

Even in the dim light in the drawing-room with the curtains drawn shut Etta could see that Fanny was decidedly ill at ease and very far from being her usual welcoming hostess.

Embarrassed at how disastrously the spontaneous visit seemed to be turning out Etta blurted out: "I do really feel bad about how long it's been since I was last in touch, but like yourselves, busy, attentive landladies, somehow there's never quite enough hours in the day. You know how it is."

Before sitting down Fanny drew back the curtains, then said: "Busy? Yes. I did wonder why, once you'd seen the announcement in the Herald, you didn't get in touch then."

The Glasgow Herald, Etta thought. *Hatches, matches, and dispatches. Well, Dolina's age would rule out births. Dolina must after all have 'set her cap' at Callum Cunningham.*

"Yes, it was all very sudden," Fanny said.

"Sudden?" Etta echoed. "I'd hardly call it that. Dolina met Callum – you both did – years ago when I first came to live here."

Fanny frowned. "What has Callum to do with anything? No, that's an unfair ungrateful thing to say. He's been a really good friend over the years, but especially after the funeral even though he had to go abroad on business he arranged for his housekeeper to look after me at his holiday home in Helensburgh –"

"Funeral? But what ... when?"

"Yes, funeral. What on earth did you think we were talking about? A bleak miserable day in February it was."

With tears in her eyes Etta looked at Fanny. "Oh, my dear, had I even known, had I had the slightest inkling that Dolina was ill, then, of course, I would have made time to visit my old friend."

"Time you say? Poor Dolina didn't have the luxury of time even to say a last farewell to anyone. She went to bed one night and just didn't wake up in the morning."

"Can you ever forgive me?"

"Forgive, yes. Forget? No. Dolina and I met many 'takers' on life's journey. We thought you were different. Nobody likes to feel they've been used. Now, if you'll excuse me. I am expecting some friends to tea later this afternoon, so ..."

As the door closed behind her, Etta found herself once again out in the baking heat of the July afternoon.

In the days following her confrontation with Fanny, Etta could not get the unhappy situation out of her mind. Time weighed heavy with her lodgers still away and no word as yet from Violet as to when she would return to her duties at Rowanbrae.

Had she also lost the friendship of Callum Cunningham? Etta wondered. Fanny had said he'd gone abroad immediately after the funeral. *Perhaps he is still away. Should I leave a message for him at his town house? No! I've never depended on any man in my entire life so why should I start now?*

Get a grip, girl. Clean out the boxroom, polish the silver. Do something, anything to keep yourself occupied. When the girls get back from their holidays they'll be so full of their adventures that will surely take you mind off your woes.

TWENTY FOUR

In the time that had passed since the traumatic visit to Fanny a great deal had changed in Etta's business and social circles.

Three of her favourite lodgers had married and although other equally pleasant young girls had occupied the self-same rooms, somehow Etta never had the same rapport with them and it was never again quite as enjoyable as it had been in the early days. Now, this letter from Violet announcing she would be staying in Arran after her Granny's death and not returning to Rowanbrae certainly completely dampened the enthusiasm which had buoyed Etta up and brought success in her first years as a landlady.

Deep in thought, oblivious to the crowds around her, Etta collided with a young woman. Each stepped back to apologise then gasped in surprise.

"I don't believe it after all this time." It was Una, one of Etta's first lodgers.

They hugged and Etta said: "I was just heading for afternoon tea. Please join me."

As they chatted and reminisced Una commented that the tearoom's confectionaries fell far below the standard of Violet's spongecake and shortbread.

"Strange you should mention Violet. She inherited a big old house in Arran from her Granny and she's been over there settling matters. It seems the house needs all sort of major repairs so Violet is debating whether to sell the house and take a smaller place in Arran.

"The thing is what she would really like to do is to get the essential repairs done and run it as a holiday guest-house but ... only on one condition ..."

Una smiled. "Let me guess, she wants you to go into a business partnership with her."

"Yes, exactly right. And I'm certainly tempted. Glasgow has now lost the charm it once had for me. But enough blethers about me and my concerns. What have you been up to since you left Rowanbrae?"

Sadly, Una's tale was soon told. She had been very happy in her marriage and had a son, Rowan, now four, but her husband had died in a whisky-bond warehouse fire Etta remembered reading about. She was now living with her mother-in-law, who, grief-stricken, wallowing in her own misery, unable to let go of the past, made an unhealthy companion for a young widow and an energetic toddler.

Sitting alone in Rowanbrae later that evening Etta came to a decision.

Right, high time I spent a bit of money on myself and those I care about. I'll take Una and wee Rowan to Arran with me for a wee holiday. We'll meet up with Violet. Have a look at her Granny's old house, consider the possibilities ... and we'll just take it from there.

It can't have been an accident bumping into Una today. If we three women go into business together we'll make a success of it – beholden to no man!

TWENTY FIVE

1874

As Etta , Una and Rowan stood at the boat's rail, Una gave a shout of delight as she pointed to the figure of a woman who was standing rather too near the edge of the pier for her own safety.

"Look, Etta, look, there she is, it's Violet. Violet, here we are, yoohoo yoohoo."

At the sudden hullabaloo, Rowan, who although he could see nothing out of the ordinary to get excited about, started to jump about, demanding to be lifted on high, At once Etta lifted the child in her arms and whispered to him: "Wave a hand, Rowan, there's a good boy, wave a hand and say hello to your Auntie Violet."

As his chubby hand waved, he, then caught up in the excitement, started chanting: "Auntie, Auntie Vyet, Auntie Auntie Vyet."

An elderly matron, standing nearby and one whose own family had doubtless long gone from her home and fireside, smiled fondly at this impromptu demonstration of childish exuberance and said: "Uch, the wee soul is that no lovely? He's just that fair excited tae see his Auntie again."

Una turned to face the woman, nodded and said: "Oh aye, he's excited all right, he's never been on a Clyde ferry before, never even been out of Glasgow, and come to that, my son has never clapped eyes on his Auntie Violet in his life."

"Uch the wee soul. Disnae even know her frae Adam, and areddies, he's got his very ain pet name for her."

On cue and clearly enjoying every minute of the extra attention being rained on him. Rowan yet again took up his chant of: "Auntie, Auntie Vyet, Auntie Auntie Vyet."

Wiping a slowly trickling tear from her rheumy eyes, the old woman laid a hand on Una's jacketed arm. " Would ye just listen tae the wee pet. Ah don't suppose Ah've been the first person tae tell ye this, but you and your man can be real proud o that clever wee bairn. He's a clever, braw wee bairn. and that's a fact."

Una had to swallow hard a couple of times before finally managing to reply: "Thank you, yes, as you say, I am indeed proud of my wee boy, but sadly, I'll be bringing him up on my own. His Daddy was killed, yon terrible distillery fire, inferno, more like."

Again the old woman's face clouded. "Aw, listen, hen, Ah didnae mean tae upset ye. But seeing yer wee laddie, it brought back happy memories of my ain family, but the years move on, just a damn shame they become adults and grow away from ye. That's life, I suppose."

"Aye, one way another, it's a strange life, I'd never have thought for a moment that I'd be rearing Rowan on my own."

As Una's voice trailed away leaving so many other words and feelings unsaid, Etta handed over to her the still-frantically waving son with the words: "Bringing up that wee rascal on your own, stuff and nonsense. You'll have Violet and me to help you."

Una wheeled round and Etta went on to say: "And what's more, his upbringing will be here on this lovely Island."

Una's eyes opened wide in amazement. "But we ... we haven't ... nothing's been decided ... a holiday you said, nothing more, an initial visit to let us see the lie of the land."

Etta grinned like a naughty schoolgirl rather than the ageing matron she acknowledged that she now was and said: "It's thanks to this lady and her helpful comments I've made up my mind. The three of us, you, me and Violet, we'll all care for wee Rowan."

Then turning to their fellow passenger, Etta went on: "We're heading for Gorsehill House. In the village of Corrie, I believe."

The old woman nodded and her face brightened. "Oh Gorsehill House, I know it well, I've been coming to Arran for years now, I always rent a front-house for the duration of the Glasgow Fair. Often old Mrs. Moss, a kindly lady, would have me up to the big House for afternoon tea. But she died a few years back and I haven't been on the Island since then. I suppose by now the lovely old House will be an empty shell. The march of time yet again."

Etta smiled: "Our friend Violet you see still teetering on the edge of the pier, she inherited the place. And once it's up and running again, let me tell you, you will be our first guest. My name by the way is Etta Duncan and you are ...?"

"Mrs Watt, but most people in Corrie know me, so just ask for Martha Watt from Hyndland, that'll find me And, of course, I'd love to see Gorsehill House again."

On that happy note Una, Etta and Rowan arrived on the Isle of Arran, on the island's first pier, only two years old, to the skirl of the pipes, the screech of the seagulls and a riotous, emotional welcome from Violet.

They travelled by pony and trap from Brodick to the village of Corrie, and it was but a short distance up a slight incline from the shore-hugging road to Gorsehill House. As they entered the pillared porch way, Etta could see at first glance that although attempts had been made to have the entrance clean and tidy it was clear even to the most untrained of housekeepers that much still remained to be done. Once inside the vast hall with its high ceilings, broken cornices, flaking paint and cracked floor tiles, all told their own story. Violet, keenly aware of Etta's inspection. quickly ushered her friends into a room which led off the almost baronial hall.

She waved her guests to seats, and with a faintly apologetic smile said: "My dear old Granny always referred to this as the Drawing Room."

As Etta and Una gazed around them, Una remarked: "It's certainly stately enough for such a grand sounding title. And what a view of the sweeping lawns, I don't think I've ever before been in a room with ceiling-to-floor massive windows."

Violet laughed. "Thank you for such kind comments, but as for the sweeping lawns, from the state of them right now they look rather more of a jungle."

On hearing this, Rowan, who'd been sitting quietly and clearly somewhat in awe of his surroundings, revived and yelled in full voice: "Jungle, jungle. Mammy, me want to see monkeys, lions and tigers"

The three women burst out laughing and his mother said: "Rowan, it's not really a jungle, son, Auntie Violet was just joking."

Violet lifted the immediately crestfallen tot onto her lap. "That's right, son, no monkeys nor even one roaring big lion lurking out there. But there is something better ... here let me whisper to you what I did find hidden away in the mass of bushes."

Cupping a hand round her mouth she let him into the secret.

His eyes widened in wonder and in his excitement he stuttered: "A boat, a real boat, honestly Auntie Vyet?"

She nodded. "And what's more, Rowan, if your Mammy agrees, later on you could go out and play in it."

He grinned and grinned even more when his Aunt said: "Better still, I've got a real ship Captain's bunnet for you, I found it up in the loft. So one way and another you can be the Captain of the good ship Gorsehill Ferry. You'd like that wouldn't you?"

Rowan's beaming face told its own story of joyful acceptance and never backward at coming forward, he pushed his luck saying: "Well, Auntie, Vyet, if I'm the Captain, does that mean I can have jeelie pieces for my tea?"

She patted his head. "You can have anything you want, Captain, sir, anything you want."

In that moment, Etta knew it was going to be all right, they had all made the right decision ... they had in a sense come home to exactly the place they were meant to be. The only immediate danger she could foresee was that as the focus of too much attention, adoration and love between the three of them they might end up by spoiling Rowan and he would end up as an insufferable spoilt brat, who thought the world started and ended with him.

But then she thought: *Could any child ever have too much love bestowed on him?*

Una glanced across and with a questioning look said: "Looking rather serious, Etta, anything I can help with?"

Etta shook her head. "Just reflecting that with young Rowan as the brave illustrious Captain of our ship, soon we'll all be sailing into calm seas."

His mother laughed. "Calm seas indeed? Stormy waters more like if I know my son ... his way or no way."

TWENTY SIX

The decision to move to Arran having been taken, from then on, everything seemed to happen with the speed of light.

With the money released from the sale of Rowanbrae, nothing then stood in the way of getting the essential repairs and desired improvements done to Gorsehill House.

As the three women stood surveying the freshly-painted hall with its new furnishings of monks' bench, sturdy oaken coat rack, roll top desk and even a gleaming brass umbrella stand, they smiled, knowing that they had already achieved what even months before would have been well-nigh impossible. They had got the entrance to the grand old house exactly right.

With what seemed like a cast of hundreds of plumbers, joiners, builders and gardeners over time Gorsehill House was fast emerging as the elegant, imposing Georgian mansion it had once been. While the ongoing restoration work revealed many a hidden treasure such as one particularly ornate fireplace in a back bedroom; it also brought into the light of day such unwelcome and costly-to-put right problems like dry rot, rising damp and gaping casements.

"What next?" moaned Violet at one point. "You know, Etta, if I could have foreseen all these horrendous problems, I really don't know that I'd ever have started the project in the first place." Etta grinned: "Well, my dear girl, you or rather we three friends did start it. so now nothing else for it, but we'll just have to battle on. Don't forget, this is a road I personally have travelled before. Remember Rowanbrae? I had to do all the groundwork there and it worked out pretty well, didn't it? Look at the happiness, the comfort and above all the friendships it generated. So, believe me, I do know all the effort and the cash expenditure on Gorsehill in the end will be worth every ounce of energy and every farthing spent on it."

"You seem very sure of that."

"Sure of it, of course I am. Apart from anything else just look at the advantages so far: a truly wonderful safe haven in which to bring up Rowan; a home for us three women on our own; a coach-house for our housekeeper Fanny and husband Sam; and not to mention the amount of lucrative business we've already brought to local shopkeepers and tradesmen ... Do you want me to go on with this list?"

Violet laughed and holding up a hand in mock protest said: "No more, I beg of you, no more. Enough is enough, thanks all the same."

Just then Una came into the room with a happily chattering Rowan. In a frenzy of excitement the wee lad held out a bucketful of shells, seaweed, cockles and other such detritus from the seashore.

Violet at once bent down to examine his latest store of garnered treasure. "Who's a clever wee laddie, then, lots of lovely seashells for your collection. Look, what's this? My, my, is that even a razor shell you've found, treasure indeed?"

As his beloved Auntie Violet oohed and ahed over his morning's collection from Corrie beach, the housekeeper, Fanny, came in. She took one look at the scene and said: "So, now young Master Rowan is allowed to trail his bucket and sand-covered spade all through the house, is he?"

Rowan looked up in surprise and at once his Auntie Violet spoke for him: "Uch, Fanny, he's only a child, not doing one bit of harm what's a wee sprinkling of sand to worry about?"

Fanny gave a sigh of exasperation. "Well seen you don't do the sweeping up. Honestly, I swear to God, between the lot of youse, you'll have that wee chap ruined. Spare the rod and spoil the child, that's what I always say."

Etta grinned: "And what I always say ... what's for eating this dinnertime? If Rowan's been scavenging Corrie's foreshore all morning, stands to reason the poor wee lad could eat a horse."

TWENTY SEVEN

The renovations had been completed, the decorating done throughout the house and wiping tears of happiness from her eyes, Una said: "So now I suppose that means that Gorsehill House is open to receive paying guests?"

Violet agreed. "But first Etta has something to say on that, not so Etta?"

Etta nodded. "I think as a courtesy we should invite a non-paying guest, remember the lady we met on the ferry? It was in talking to her that day as we arrived that she helped me make up my mind that Arran, Corrie and Gorsehill House really would be the place for us."

Una nodded. "Not only that. But it would please Fanny enormously to have her Aunt Martha as guest of honour. It was, after all, the very same Martha Watt who was instrumental in matching us up with Fanny and Sam."

Violet said: "And as I recall it was just in time as we were almost on the point of demolishing the coach-house. A real pity that would have been especially knowing your great love of old buildings, Etta."

Etta smiled. "True enough. Anyway, now with its picturesque olde-worlde appearance, tubs of flowers and all, it quite definitely adds a touch of elegance, a general air of grandeur to the Big House itself. Yes, it adds to the ambience."

The discussion about the coach-house came to an end when Fanny came into the room.

"Right ladies, that's the wee laddie had his bath, now looking like a bright shining heavenly wee angel, he's listening to my hubby reading him a story. What he needs now is a wee cuddle from his Mammy before he settles to sleep."

"Honestly, Fanny," Una said, "I don't know what we'd do without you and your husband. You both give well over and above the call of duty."

The grey-haired woman smiled. "Away with you, compliments will get you everywhere. Sam and me, we're the lucky ones, landed on our feet so we did. Anyway, if Rowan's bath time was left to you three, it would be all hours of the night before he was ready for bed."

Etta assumed a mock-serious expression. "Are you saying that we are none of us competent to supervise a child's bath time?"

"What I'm saying is this ... you all make such a fuss of the wee chap, he plays up to it for all he's worth. He twists you three musketeers around his little finger."

Violet grinned: "Guilty as charged, my lady."

Fanny pointed an admonitory finger. "You, madam, Auntie Violet, you're the worst of the lot." As the laughter died away, Violet said: "Well, if I'm all that bad, I'd better try to make amends, perhaps get myself off to the kitchen, peel a pail-full of spuds. Mince-n-tatties I think you said for tonight's meal?" Their maid-of-all-work nodded "Aye, that's the menu for tonight, but ye neednae fash yersel at this late hour, I done all the preparations earlier when Rowan was out in the garden, playing at Captains. And of course, his Uncle Sam, he was the naughty cabin-boy refusing to obey the orders of the bunneted ship's Captain."

Una grinned. "Even so, Sam must have been promoted, last week he was a captured pirate being ordered to walk the plank"

In the peace and quiet after the withdrawal of Una and Fanny, Etta said: "I believe a small sherry might be a just reward for all the work we've done around the place today."

Violet grinned. "Best offer I've had all day. Seriously though, it's marvellous to see the old house coming alive again and to know that already we are so far forward with everything. I'll never be able to thank you enough, Etta."

Etta made no reply but quickly gulped back her tears. "Come to think of it, I believe a large sherry would be more to the point."

The idea of an open day with Fanny's Aunt Martha Watt as guest of honour had quickly gained approval and Etta concluded their latest discussion on the subject by saying: "Right then, a gala-day it is."

Fanny, catching fag-ends of the conversation as she entered the room, said: "A gala day indeed. Sounds like more work for yours truly."

Una hastened to say: "We'll all pitch in."

Violet rubbed her hands together in a very business-like manner. "Now we've got that out of the way, down to details. How does a day in mid-July sound, the Glasgow Fair then, isn't it?"

As over time preparations began in earnest, one day in the midst of all the flurry, Violet stopped work to say: "You know what, girls I vote for making this an annual event in Corrie's social calendar."

"Amazing to think this will be our second gala day, isn't it?"

Una looked up from the piles of sandwiches she was arranging artistically on suitably-large platters. "Aye, time flies when you're enjoying yourself. And come September, Rowan will be moving up into junior school. He settled in really well from his very first day at school ... so much for Fanny's theory about spoiling the child. Not a bit spoiled is he?"

A perfect summer day, not a cloud in the sky, the sun already strong, the local pipe band blowing their hearts out and a medley of pirates, gypsies, demure milkmaids, befrocked ships captains and fairy godmothers streaming across the front lawns. And somewhere in the middle of this fancy-dress parade, done out like an admiral of the fleet, ceremonial sword and all, young Master Rowan was in his element. Even Miss Bassett, his schoolteacher had not only admired his costume but she had actually congratulated him on his brilliant idea.

"Yes, Rowan, how very clever of you to suggest a fancy-dress theme for this year's Gala Day. After all, it's not very often that I get the chance to appear in public not as a Lochgelly-wielding school-ma'am but rather as a wand-waving fairy godmother, now is it?"

She moved away to join her Irish washerwoman-garbed sister, and Rowan, face aglow, was clearly still basking in such fulsome praise when his mother, Aunt Etta and Auntie Violet arrived at his side.

"Looking mighty pleased with yourself, young man, or should I say Admiral?"

Spotting an older pupil from the class above his own, a known bully whose only fancy dress was an old tweed bunnet and a long white scarf, Rowan sidled in closer to his mother.

She patted his hand. "What say we make our way over to the trestle tables, there's everything there from petticoat tails of shortbread, potato-scones, Empire biscuits ... you name it and even sherry-trifle for the adults and clootie-dumplin for those who're still bairns at heart."

As they passed by Workman Dugald, the latter stuck out his tongue and made his eyes go skelly at the sight of the richly-dressed Admiral of the Fleet.

Although having quickly averted his eyes from the grotesque faces being made at him, Rowan was near enough the 'workman' to be in no doubt as to what the other was chanting at him, all the while wagging his head in time to the definite beat, the rhythm of his hateful composition. "Teacher's pet, got his troosers wet, Mammy's bairnie cannae stop his streamie, teacher's pet, got his troosers wet, teacher's pet I'll get you yet."

Rowan gasped and quickly looked up at his mother to see if she had heard the vile accusation. But she was striding purposefully towards the food.

However, his Auntie Violet frowned. "What was that horrible child saying just now? Couldn't quite catch it, but I'm sure it was something cheeky or hurtful to somebody. Anyway, he'd better watch out making grotesque faces like that, his face might stick like that, then where would he be?"

She frowned over at the boy, then laughing down at Rowan she said: "Well, Admiral, as your Aunt Etta would say, after commanding your fleet all morning, I'm sure you could just about eat a horse."

And laughing happily together, they left the bully Dugald to his own devices, to go and pester somebody else, preferably a weaker boy who did not have a posse of adoring aunts to protect him.

TWENTY EIGHT

The new school term was scarcely a couple of months old and already the previously always keen-to-go-to-school Rowan was making feeble excuses each morning as to why he should stay in bed and nurse a supposedly sick headache. Having endured this useless strategy for days on end now, his mother appealed to Etta.

"I can't get a thing out of him, he says nothing's wrong. He likes his teacher, he can manage his sums, his times tables and even his mental arithmetic and spelling tests. Etta, would you have a word with him?"

Etta nodded. "Sounds to me like a bad case of bullying. On reflection perhaps the gold-emblazoned fancy costume at the gala day was a mistake? Lots of other children, from poorer cottages in the village had to make do with the odd bit of tartan, a hand-me-down kilt, a workman's bunnet ... wait a minute, yes, I do recall something. Yes, of course, I'll have a word with him, don't worry Una, we'll get to the bottom of this."

A few evenings later, with Rowan safely in bed, Etta said: "Just as we suspected, a case of sour grapes and a concerted attempt to bully our Rowan. Stupid chanting at him in the playground, that kind of thing. Anyway I've had a word with Dorothy Bassett over the teacups. Now she is aware of the unhappy situation, it will not be happening again."

Una breathed a sigh of relief. "Thank heavens for that. Children can be very cruel to each other, can't they? I just cannot imagine what on earth they could have been chanting to get him in such a sorry state?"

Etta looked down, and said not a word but studied her fingernails as if her life depended on such intense examination.

Una gasped. "You know, you know what they said, so come on, out with it, Etta."

Etta raised her head. "You won't like it, any more than poor Rowan did. But if you insist..."

Una tightened her lips. "I do. I do insist."

Etta sat up straighter in her chair. "All right, here goes and please don't say I didn't warn you. It was something along the lines of, 'Rowan, cowan, bastard lad, Rowan, cowan, hasnae got a dad ...' and so on ad infinitum. You get the picture I'm sure."

Total silence greeted this sing-song performance of the hated, spiteful bile.

Into this uneasy silence walked Violet with the cheerful greeting: "Something I should know about?"

Once the story had been related to her, the resourceful Violet sat meditating for some time before at last saying: "You know, several points arising from this ... in future we must not spoil Rowan quite so much, must make him stand on his own feet. After all a mummy's boy is one thing, but don't forget he's got three of us on his case. And Rowan aside, something else. It's been on my mind for some time. Now that our bed-n-breakfast trade is doing so well, perhaps there could be an element of jealousy also from some local grownups, do you think? I'm sure the Corrie Hotel has lost business to us. And not forgetting all the locals who rent out their front houses in the season, what about them?"

"Of course, the age-old Arran tradition, people moving into their back-garden but-n-bens and renting out the front house. But now if more and more holidaymakers prefer to stay at Gorsehill?"

Una put a hand to her mouth. "You know, you're right, last thing we want to do alienate the locals, destroy the good relations we've built up over the years. Come to think of it, those new owners of the hotel, gave me a very frosty good morning recently."

Etta stood up. "You and me both, so what's to do now before the locals start up a chant about us?"

Nothing like it had ever before been suggested, far less tried out on Arran.

Etta's idea of activity and leisure interests holiday not only brought even greater business to Gorsehill House, but it meant that in catering for an entirely different type of clientele in no way were they stepping on the toes of any other hoteliers, guest house owners or householders renting out their front houses. During any fancy-baking weekends, Violet was in her element revealing her culinary secrets as she demonstrated the finer points of shortbread making and light-as-a-feather, heavenly meringues. On the home cookery events, it would be Fanny's turn to shine when eager participants would try their 'prentice hands at such Scottish dishes as Cullen Skink, stovies and the ever-popular clootie dumplins.

When it came to antiques, Etta cast herself in the role of tutor advisor as she happily shared her hard-won knowledge of Wemyss pottery, Mauchline ware and Irish Baleek china.

For anyone with a burning desire to make their very own wooden porridge spurtle, a creepie stool or even a hand-carved doll's cot, then Sam would be drafted in from his beloved and now always immaculate Gorsehill gardens to hold his master-classes in woodworking.

Not to be left out of things, young Rowan was put in charge of the shop, a card table in the hall on which was displayed a variety of hand knitted goods, postcards, and slabs of Violet's vanilla tablet.

One Saturday morning, as Rowan was getting ready to replenish his stock of goods on the sales table. Etta, wishing to be helpful, came in from the kitchen bearing a heavy tray of the latest offerings. Seeing this, with her walking stick in one hand and the tray balanced somewhat precariously in the other, Rowan at once rushed to her side.

"Here, Aunt Etta, let me take that from you, you shouldn't be carrying heavy things like that at your age."

Etta relinquished her hold on the tray, then feeling more tired than she cared to admit to anyone, she hobbled over to the nearest seat, the monks' bench.

As she sat down, she cast a speculative look at Rowan and said: 'Thank you for your assistance, Rowan, but honestly, I was managing perfectly well on my own."

He gave a cheeky grin. "If you say so, but hundreds wouldn't believe you."

Etta gave a rueful smile. "I've always said throughout my life, that I have need of no man to help me but then as you so kindly pointed out ... perhaps now at my great age ..."

Rowan laughed. "Now you're making fun of me, Aunt Etta. First of all I'm not a man yet, a long way still to go in my growing up and honestly I never mentioned anything about a great age."

Etta rose stiffly to her feet. "We'll leave that flea stick to the wall. But you have given me food for thought."

TWENTY NINE

1884

Una, Violet, Fanny and Sam were all assembled in the drawing room and as they awaited the arrival of Etta, Fanny said, half-fun, half earnest: "You don't suppose she wanted us gathered together in here to announce that she's decided to sack Sam and me and then purloin the coach-house for herself for her twilight years?"

Just at that Etta entered, for once minus her walking stick and looking more elegant, more erect and more determined than she had of late.

"Fanny, I couldn't help overhearing what you said, so right now let me put everyone's mind at rest. There will be no sackings, and no purloining of your home. As for that emotive phrase, twilight years, if you'll pardon my French ... bugger that."

There was a startled gasp and a thumbs-up gesture from Sam who gave a hearty laugh and to Fanny's annoyance said: "Amen to that, Mistress Duncan! Always knew you had a navvy's turn of phrase when it suited you."

Etta laughed. "That's for me to know, and you to wonder about, but any more of this, and watch out, bonnie lad, but you will be getting your marching orders."

As the laughter died away, Violet said: "Etta, is there any point to all of this, I've got a stack of work still to get through this morning. So why did you call this meeting? If that's what it's supposed to be."

Etta looked at each one of them in turn then said: "Just recently, and although I do hate to admit it, but I have been feeling my age, what with stiff bones, less energy and I've realised that being as comfortable and cosseted as I am here with all of you, even young Rowan nowadays rushing to help me carry so much as a tray, well, it suddenly brought home to me the fact that ... I am hugely blessed, indeed I am. But if I stay on here like this with all of you more and more waiting hand and foot over me, then despite myself, it would be too easy to sit back and wallow in such luxury, such comfort. In other words, I'd be allowing myself to become old."

Violet burst in: "Can we stop this right now, Etta? All right, you are getting old, we all are, but there's nothing anyone of us can do about that."

Fanny got to her feet. "Mistress Duncan, Etta, do you mind if I say something ... the fact is although you might still see yourself as some young mill girl, the fact is, yes, you are an old woman, no shame to that and if we all want to spoil you a bit in old age, surely no harm there either?"

Etta smiled. "Yes, I knew it, just knew you'd all want to spoil me rotten, just what I was afraid of and while in many ways I'd love it … who wouldn't … even so, I'm convinced it would only hasten my descent into a useless old age. So, thank you, but no thank you. Now I want you all to calm down, listen to my plans."

Etta cleared her throat: "It's like this and what I'm about to say may well surprise you, because I was beginning to wonder if ever I'd have the courage to go ahead with my master plan. Recently, I had a an insurance life policy mature, I never thought I'd live long enough to see the day, but now I have and –"

Fanny interrupted. "A shopping trip to the Mainland, spend your ill-gotten gains, something like that?"

Etta smiled. "No, a bit more ambitious than that. For the first time in my life, I'm going to spend every halfpenny on me, I've signed on for a round-the-world trip on a cargo ship. Yes, I could afford a luxury liner, but that's not what I have in mind. I've had enough of pretence and dressing up to last me for this lifetime."

Total, stunned silence greeted this announcement and then everybody started talking at once with questions, objections, denials, but Etta was having none of it.

"You can all stop right there, my mind is made up, my plans are finalized, and I'm due to join my ship at Greenock in ten days' time."

At once Sam said: "In that case, Mistress Duncan, I will escort you over to Greenock."

Etta stared hard at him. "Isn't that what I've been talking about, Sam? I don't mean to be rude, but if you would see me to the Arran ferry at Brodick, I'll then be off on my travels alone. You see, Greenock port was once the start of a new life for me, and even though I'm old, I do still feel I have a lot of living to do. So, please, please be happy for me and wish me bon voyage for this next phase of my life."

The End

Also by Jenny Telfer Chaplin:

The Candleriggs Trilogy

Beyond the Bridge of Time

A Life to Live in Glasgow

Published by Bewrite Books

Available as Ebooks from www.Bewrite.net and through Amazon and Barnes& Noble

A Daughter is for Life

Set in Her Ways

Rich Tapestry of a Tangled Life

Published by Kinnon Enterprises

Available in print from www.Lulu.com and through Amazon and Barnes & Noble.